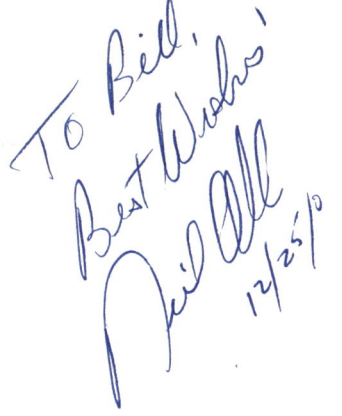

A SYMPHONY TO FINISH

NEIL ALLEN

PublishAmerica
Baltimore

© 2004 by Neil Allen.
All rights reserved. No part of this book may be reproduced, stored in a retrieval system or transmitted in any form or by any means without the prior written permission of the publishers, except by a reviewer who may quote brief passages in a review to be printed in a newspaper, magazine or journal.

First printing

ISBN: 1-4137-3895-8
PUBLISHED BY PUBLISHAMERICA, LLLP
www.publishamerica.com
Baltimore

Printed in the United States of America

This book is dedicated to my mother, Pauline, my father, Abe, and all of the other wonderful people along my way who had more confidence in my potential and me than I had in myself. It wasn't until much later that I realized that their persistent pushing was driven totally by love. My wish is that they know how much I appreciate them and love them now.

First and foremost I want to thank my new wife of fourteen years, Karen, for her support, encouragement, and help in making this possible for me.

I thank my son, Neil Jr. and LauraLeigh for providing the fuel of encouragement that helped keep me going so that I could meet the deadline!

A special acknowledgment to my three feline fur persons not only for their technical advice but for helping me during my moments of author's block by hitting the proper keystrokes on my keyboard with their adept paws. I hope that their concerns of being followed by the paw-purr-azzi are unfounded.

I want to acknowledge and thank Ron Huber, author of A Ward of the State for being a great friend and for urging me to complete my book that had been sitting idle for a long time in a drawer and in my head. I would like to especially thank him for all of his guidance through the process.

I want to thank Daniel Merliss for helping me to see that my dreams can indeed come true and for giving me the tools to make it happen.

Special thanks to Thao Nguyen, a close friend and photographer, who took the photo for the back cover.

Thanks to my "onliest and bestest pal," Bobby, who has been like the brother that I never had and helped me to title this work.

HISTORICAL FILE FOOTAGE
LATE 1970S
PART 1

CHAPTER 1

There it goes. The last sound that you want to hear on a still dark and cold winter morning at 4:00 AM. This is the middle of the night, for Christ sake. *If that goddamned alarm clock doesn't shut the hell up I'm gonna throw it through the fucking window.*

Of course these words were not heard anywhere except the inside of his skull since Nick was still in that sleep state between consciousness and dreamland. The flannel sheet and down comforter were pulled tightly around his neck and clenched tightly in his hands. His body was in the fetal position, lying on his left side. With what seemed like a great effort, Nick slowly opened his right eye just enough to see the digital numbers *4:05* glaring in a green that gave the room an eerie ghostly glow. Without changing body position, Nick turned his head over his shoulder as far as he could to see if Susan was there. Nick's wife, Susan, fast asleep in a similar position only with her back to his, was undisturbed by the alarm. She didn't have to worry about being late for work, since she worked for Daddy, and could show up any time she damn well pleased. A bomb could go off next to her head, and she wouldn't blink an eye. After all, she just got home a couple of hours ago after closing Wilder's Place, a popular country western club over the river, one of the first in the area to have the newest country and western bar amusement, the mechanical bull. She said she was going out with the girls. At least that was the message that Nick retrieved from the answering machine after returning home from work and picking up their son the previous afternoon around 3:30 PM.

Nick slowly rolled upright to a sitting position and reached down under the bed for his slippers. Cold bathroom tiles are an unpleasant way to wake up, not that there is any pleasant way to wake up that early in the morning. Running on automatic, Nick dragged ass over to the closet, reached in and plucked his worn out, but just broke in comfortable, blue terry robe from the hook that was screwed into the jamb on the left side. The robe was relocated to a similar hook on the back of the master bedroom's bathroom door. He reached into the shower and turned on the hot water full blast and stood on the dry side of the sliding glass door waiting for the water to reach the proper temperature. There's nothing worse than the shock of getting hit with the ice cold water that lived in the pipes over night, waiting to be evicted by the force of the hot water. The shower was quick, mostly just for a wake up and to remove the bed hair look. After a quick shave, Nick dressed in his usual dark slacks, white shirt and tie—required dress at the television station where he worked as a technician.

The monogrammed black blazer, also part of the uniform, was grabbed from the door knob on his way to the kitchen where he retrieved his keys from the top of the fridge. Nick grabbed his winter coat and gloves, and within 20 minutes after first opening his eyes, was in his new 1978 Mustang, and on the road to "sign on" one of the local network affiliated television stations.

Normally Nick's mind ran on automatic, but this morning was different. A new technician was starting today and that always added some new excitement to what was normally a pretty mundane broadcast day. What added even more excitement was the fact that this new technician was a woman. A female television technician was a very rare thing these days. There were still a lot of *fossils* working at the station who started working there when the cameras were powered by coal. They referred to you as the FNG, fuckin' new guy, even if you'd worked there for ten years. Now these same fossils not only had a fuckin' new technician to deal with but a female at that. Nick knew that this would bring out the "keep the broads out of broadcasting" sentiments. Sometimes it was great fun to watch the old guys squirm as new, young, and talented technicians came on board.

CHAPTER 2

As the Mustang pulled into the employee parking lot at the back of the station, the horizon was becoming a blend of amber and blue as the sun began to rise. Nick pulled into one of the 10 spaces reserved for engineering, shut off the engine, and stepped out. The biting cold wind stung his face. The station was only a few blocks from the river, which always made it feel colder than in the suburbs. The memory of past incidents of car lights left on or keys locked securely inside the car after the occupant had exited, prompted him to make one last feel of the keys in his pocket and take a glance at the lights before shutting the door and continuing on. From the look of the nearly empty parking lot, he was the first tech to arrive. The only other cars in the lot were those belonging to "Mannix," the 70-some-odd-year-old security guard (whose namesake was that of the current and popular T.V. sleuth) stationed at the employee entrance, and the overnight reporter in the news room whose main job was to listen to the police and fire scanners for any overnight action that anyone might give a shit about by noon. Nick sprinted past the heliport to the back entrance of the building which was mainly used for employees and deliveries. At this hour Mannix was often found fast asleep at the switchboard, head down on his left forearm, and right hand on his pistol which was lying on the desk. All of the technicians had keys, but one was always careful not to startle Mannix into action and thereby making oneself the top story on the Noon Report.

Nick already had his key in hand and quietly unlocked the outer door. Mannix slowly raised his head and rubbed his eyes. He had a large red spot on his forehead from where it rested on his arm.

"Eh, Nick. Good mornin'. Cold as a well digger's asshole out there, ain't it?"

"Yeah, no shit. Shoot any bad guys last night?"

Mannix's major activity of the night was most likely the frequent inspection of the inside of his eyelids.

Mannix laughed, "That's pretty good. So, how's the old lady?"

He had been introduced to Susan once before, at one of the company Christmas parties. She was a "looker" with shoulder length blonde hair that was slightly on the auburn side and a great body. Easy to remember.

"She's 'bout as cold as it is outside. Thanks for asking."

Nick walked through the newsroom to the stairs toward the back that went up to the technical operations area. The only sounds were the whir of the air conditioning, the crackling of the police and fire radios, and the clacking of the UPI and AP teletype machines. No sight of the news dude. He sprinted up the steps, and at the top he turned left into the video tape, projection, and Master Control area known as tele-cine. The tele-cine area was affectionately known as the "sausage factory." Just like stuffing sausage every day.

Nick's first stop was the maintenance shop area where the large daily schedule sheet was located. Today he was scheduled to work the projection/master switcher position. After signing in, he went over to the projection side of tele-cine. Sitting on the projection desk was the daily program log which listed in chronological order every program to be aired, commercial advertisements, public service announcement or station promotional announcements, and the times at which they had to air. Nick made the commercial changes from the "change sheet," circled the slides, and then began pulling the first couple hours worth of slides from the drawers located in the wall directly behind him. Holding the slides by the edges, he placed the slide in his opened mouth, huhed his moist breath on them, and wiped the past day's fingerprints from them with a towel that was tied by the corner to a big metal loop dangling from the table. After loading the first of the program slides in the slide projectors and the first film reels on the projectors, Nick went into the Master Control booth to get the remotely operated transmitter fired up.

Meanwhile, Alan, the second technician assigned to the sign-on shift arrived. He was assigned to video tape, which was in the vicinity of the tele-cine, directly across from the projection area and adjacent to the glass enclosed master control booth. Using a copy of the same program log, Alan was responsible for loading the video taped programs and commercials on the four large reel-to-reel video tape machines and one video tape cartridge machine.

"Pretty fuckin' cold, huh Nick? Sorry I'm a little late, but I had trouble getting that old piece of shit of mine to turn over this morning."

Nick couldn't let this one pass by. "You mean your wife or the Chevy?"

"Cute. The car's running fine, asshole. Nobody talks about my car that way, get it?"

They both laughed.

"I'm gonna put *Sunrise Semester* on 15 and go take a shit," Alan said through sips of Dunkin Doughnut coffee.

"Thanks for sharing that. You didn't bring any extra doughnuts with ya, did ya?"

"Sure, they're in the bag under the tape counter. Help yourself."

The transmitter was located several miles away but was operated by remote control. Nick turned on the appropriate switches in the proper sequence and watched as the color bars appeared on the program monitor and the test tone was heard on the speakers. Within minutes the master control director, Herman, had arrived. Herman was one of the staff announcers who doubled as the sign-on director, the "other duties as assigned" part of his job description. Herman played trumpet in a dance band in his spare time and practiced playing the trumpet in the men's room between commercial breaks while long program segments were airing. The acoustics made him feel like he was playing Carnegie Hall. During the Korean War, some twenty years earlier, Herman, as a youth in his late teens, was in the Marine Corps Band. Not such a cushy gig as you might think. The band was also responsible for collecting the casualties from the battlefield.

Herman called for a roll and take of projector one on film chain seven, which Nick executed on the master control audio follow video switcher. The national anthem was on the air, and a new program day had begun. It was 5:20 AM.

After the National Anthem was aired and the first program on the air, Nick had 28 minutes to help himself to one of Alan's cinnamon twist yeast doughnuts—his favorite—and to begin his search for a cup of coffee. The good news was that there was always an industrial sized coffee urn in the maintenance shop. The not so good news was that its contents were left over from the sign-off shift which left three hours ago and probably still contained some of yesterday's coffee. Everyone liked having the coffee pot, but no one wanted to clean it or make the next brew after taking the last drop. There was enough of the sludge for one cup. Not too bad when cut with some hot water from the men's room tap, three heaping teaspoons of sugar and a mound of Creamora powder. The specific gravity of the tar colored ooze was such that the Creamora didn't even sink to the bottom. "Ahh, good shit." Nick said, in a way that might better describe a good shot of Southern Comfort. Actually, a shot of Southern Comfort right now would have been great for a couple of reasons.

CHAPTER 3

Around 8:30 the "normal" day shift technicians began arriving, as did the Chief Engineer, Malloy. Malloy was a great natured man of slight build with thinning reddish blond hair that he combed back on the sides. He had worked at the station since the early 50s, starting as a technician and working himself up to position of chief. Malloy was soft spoken and not a micro-manager. The console in tele-cine was just across the hall and in direct line of sight of Malloy's office. After performing his morning administrative duties, Malloy strolled across the hall and stood next to Nick. He called over to Alan, who was at the tape counter working the crossword puzzle, a morning ritual not to be messed with.

"Hey Alan, Nick. Can you guys come over here a minute?" Malloy called. "I have to give you guys a heads up about something."

"What's up, Chief?" Alan replied, wiping the last crumb of doughnut from his face onto the sleeve of his right arm.

"As you probably have heard, unless you have been vacationing on Mars or smoking McFried's cigarettes, we have a young woman technician starting today. I know, or at least confident that you two, being FNG's yourselves, (Nick was in his ninth year and Alan his fifth) will make her feel at home and show her the ropes. It goes without saying, but I'll say it anyway, watch those potty mouths of yours around her, especially you," he said as he lowered his head and looked over his half glasses directly toward Alan.

"Ok? And by the way, Alan, do you actually put food in that filthy mouth of yours?"

"I'll try but no guarantees. It's a hard habit to break, especially around here," Nick replied.

He looked into Malloy's eyes and saw that signature twinkle and could swear that he could see the corners of his mouth breaking a smile. Malloy started towards the control room area.

"Now for the hard part. I have to give the same spiel to the rest of F-Troop. Thanks for letting me practice my lines on you guys."

He lowered his head and walked off. Alan and Nick resumed their mundane tasks of putting 'em up and taking 'em down. Roll it, take it, you know, the same old shit. Just another day in the "sausage factory."

CHAPTER 4

Her name was Lori. She arrived bright and eager to start her new job as a TV technician. Her previous job was at a small station in the state capitol area where she worked for about a year as an entry level, vacation relief technician. Her interest in broadcast technical work was due to the fact that her father was in the biz. Actually, her father was on the other side of the cameras as a musical performer. The rumors were already circulating that she was somehow connected to the station's general manager through her father and therefore all hands OFF.

After his lunch break, Nick settled into the chair at Master Control. Someone else had taken on the projection duties. He checked the log for upcoming network cut-ins. He had several minutes before the mid break of The Edge of Night, so he checked with Phil, his relief at the projection side of tele-cine.

"Phil, where is the P and G spot loaded?" he asked.

"It's on projector two, ID slide on nine," Phil replied.

Nick wrote the numbers on the program log, then checked the transmitter log to see if it was time for the twice per hour parameter check, assuring that all of the transmitter readings were within the FCC guidelines. He had about fifteen minutes. At 1:29:20 PM, the system cue was aired by the network, and Nick rolled the spot. Thirty seconds later he took the promo ID slide on chain nine and hit the ID cart. Back to the net at first video. After logging the times on the Official Program Log, he could feel the presence of someone behind him. He turned and saw a beautiful young woman standing there. Her hair was brunette, a little longer than shoulder length, she had big brown eyes, and a young shapely body. She appeared to be in her 20s, which would make her about 12 years younger than Nick. At first sight Nick couldn't help but to find her rather attractive.

"Hi, my name is Lori."

"Welcome aboard. My name is Nick."

Lori's eyes opened quite wide with awe as she looked around at all of the buttons, lights, and monitors in the small master control booth.

"I can't believe how much more stuff there is here than the place I came from. It will take me forever to get all of this!"

"Not really," Nick said assuredly, "Just take it one piece at a time and you'll get it in no time. For the first six weeks that I was here I wondered if I had learned *anything* at my first job. Then like a light going on, I got it."

Lori smiled and gave a little sigh of relief. Nick rose out of his chair and stood beside Lori.

"The next break is pretty simple. Just a film, slide, and ID cart. Want to do it?"

"Are you serious? I just got here."

"Don't worry; I won't let you fuck it up."

As soon as the word left his lips, the OH SHIT sign flashed brightly in his mind's eye. What he wouldn't have given for an audio reject button right now.

"I'm really sorry. That just slipped out."

"Don't worry about it. I have three brothers, so there isn't much that I haven't heard or even said myself."

"I'm still pretty embarrassed. What say I get you an I'm sorry soda after the break?"

"You've got a date. Do you really want me to do the next break? If I screw it up a million people will see it!"

"And a minute later no one will give a shit. We'll just do a make-good on Sunday afternoon. That's what those bad movies are for. Make-Good Matinee."

They both laughed.

"Besides, I will be right behind you and talk you through it. Herman is the director, so it will be fun."

"Okay. Just don't let me fuck it up."

Nick saw a devilish twinkle in her eyes, and he knew that this was going to be just fine.

"Here. Sit down and get the feel of the place and see where everything is. It's the same stuff that you worked with before, just in a different place. We'll be using projector two, so hit the red button where it says PROJ. #2."

As soon as Lori hit the button she heard a clunking sound, as the mirror in the multiplexer aimed the lens of projector 2 into the film chain camera.

"Now hit the green button where it says "SLIDE 9."

This turned on the bulb in the slide projector.

"Now on the preview row of the switcher, look at "FILM 9."

When she did this, she saw that the slide was a promo slide for the 4 PM movie which corresponded with the slide called for on the program log.

"Great! Looks like we're set. Punch "FILM 7" on the preview row so we can see the film when it comes up."

Nick looked to the right into the announce booth when he saw the overhead light go on as Herman entered and shut the door. Herman looked to his left into the master control booth, smiled, and nodded his head to Lori as he sat down.

He opened the intercom key and said "Now that's the best that room has looked as long as I can remember. Of course my memory is about as long as my...ah, never mind. I hope you aren't just visiting."

Nick pushed the intercom button to the announce booth and said, "Herman, this is Lori. She's the new tech. Started today, so be nice. You have the rest of your career to show her your ass."

"A pleasure to have you aboard."

"Herman, Lori is going to do the next break so be gentle. Okay?"

"Am I ever any other way? Okay hon, tense up. We got thirty seconds to the break."

Lori felt her heart begin to pound and her mouth start to dry out. Her scalp felt tingly. All she could think of was two million eyes watching what she was about to do.

"Ten seconds." Herman said over the intercom.

Nick stood directly behind Lori with his hands poised to reach around her to push the buttons in the event that she froze.

"Here we go. Ready to roll projector one, ready to take seven," Herman directed.

Lori had her right index finger on the run button for projector one and the other index finger gently resting on the button on the program row of the video switcher.

At 1:58:55 Herman called over the intercom,

"Roll one."

Lori pressed firmly and immediately she heard the projector directly behind her start to run. In her mind's eye she pictured herself on a roller coaster ride halfway to the summit of the largest drop. She had that too late to turn back now feeling. Three seconds later, Herman called, "Take seven."

Lori pressed the button and a rush came over her as she saw her first commercial appear on the air monitor. There were two thirty second spots tied together, so she had one minute to catch her breath. Up to this time she hadn't realized that she was holding her breath. Nick found himself standing so close behind her that he could smell the sweet smell of her shampoo rising up and teasing his nose.

"You're doing great. I told you it was easy. You're almost done. Hang in there. Get ready to take the slide on nine and hit the audio cart," Nick said reassuringly.

Lori's hands were trembling. Herman called, "Ready to take nine and hit the cart." Her right index finger found its way to the run button of the cart machine and the left index finger rested on the button with the number 9 on it.

"Take nine and hit the cart," Herman called.

Like a one-two punch, Lori took 9 and hit the cart.

"Ready net. Take net," Herman called the final command of the break.

Lori took back to the network and immediately slumped into the chair as her tensed back muscles relaxed.

"Whew. That scared the shit out of me but I did good, huh?" Lori asked.

"You did great!" Nick replied. "Now all you have to do is wipe those puddles of sweat off of the switcher."

The intercom opened again and Herman spoke.

"Are you sure you never did this before? You done good! You gonna be here for the next one?"

Lori smiled and said, "I think that's all the excitement that I can handle for one day. Maybe tomorrow."

She rose from the chair, looked at Nick and said, "I sure could use that soda right now."

"You got it. Just let me get someone to cover for me before we go."

Nick held the door open for her, and they both walked out into the video tape area. "Alan, you free to cover MC for about fifteen minutes while I get her a victory soda?"

"No problem. Here's a buck. Bring me back one? And this time don't forget to bring me the change."

As Nick took the dollar from Alan's hand Alan said with a smile and a wink "You dawg. Don't forget to bring a quart of milk home to the wife and kid tonight."

"Jesus, Alan. I'm just buying a new tech a soda."

After the soda break Nick escorted Lori to Studio A, the larger of two studios, where they were setting up for a commercial production.

"I guess I'll drop you off here for a while so that you can see what goes on down here in the pits. You can find your way back up, can't you?"

"Yeah, I think so. Thanks. I'll see you in a bit."

Nick headed back up the back stairs to tele-cine carrying a soda and a smile. He couldn't remember smiling this big in a long time.

CHAPTER 5

Nick picked up the direct line to MC. "Master Control, Nick speaking."

"So, is that supposed to impress me?"

"That shit-kicker accent cold only be one person. What's up Irv?" Nick answered.

Irv was the transmitter supervisor. The thick accent was derived from his roots in western Kentucky. The transmitter techs all had very different personalities than the studio techs. Their biggest fear was that they would someday have to come down off the hill and work in the studios. For the most part they were loners who felt a closer affinity to their rig than to any human being. Their rhythm of life was the hum of the rig's components.

"Well," Irv said almost apologetically, "It's that time again. Got to do the transmitter proofs and you know what that means."

The proofs are the yearly tests of the transmitter that are required by the Federal Communications Commission to ensure that all components are operating within legal limits and at peak performance.

"Yeah, I know. Some poor sucker—I mean volunteer has to spend the night with you."

"I'd like to start tonight after sign off, if someone is willing to stay. I know this is short notice and all. You helped me last year, so why don't you cogitate on it and let me know if you're interested? You're married, so what the hell is your hurry to get home?"

Although Nick knew that Irv was just "jerking his chain," to Nick there was some real truth to it. Nick thought for a moment. He sure could use the overtime, and Susan would probably be sleeping anyway. Nick was on the sign off shift, which ended at 2:30ish, so it would mean three hours of overtime.

"Irv, let me give the old lady a call just to let her know that I won't be home 'til 6 a.m. and I'll get back to ya. You got enough Coke and chips up there for both of us?"

Irv lived on a diet of soda, cases of which he had delivered to the transmitter site every week and potato chips which were freebies from a sponsor.

"I'll stand by," Irv replied.

Before hanging up, Nick and Irv engaged in their usual friendly telephone banter.

"Hey Irv, is it true that the three Rs that they teach in Kentucky schools is readin', ritin' and route 25 north?"

"Yeah, and the reason it's so windy in Kentucky is because Ohio sucks!"

CHAPTER 6

The relationship that Nick and Susan had was less than idyllic. They had been married for four years now. When they first got married, Nick knew that there were some problem areas with their relationship but figured that as time went on they would grow together and the problems would work themselves out. In reality it was quite the opposite. Lately it seemed that as far as Susan was concerned, he couldn't do anything right. He didn't make enough money, and he wasn't home enough. The station where Nick worked was a union shop, and he got paid according to the contract. He told Susan when she said that she wanted the new house, that if they bought it, there wouldn't be any extra money for a couple of years, until his raises caught up with the expenses. Susan promised that she understood, and that she wanted the house so badly that she would make that sacrifice. They weren't in the house for two months when she demanded, "How come Shelly and Beth each get fifty dollars a week from their husbands, and you don't give me anything? I want you to ask your boss for more money."

"I told you it was going to be really tight for a couple years, and you said you understood. I'm doing the best that I can!" Nick said angrily.

The basic foundation of a good marriage, trust and communications, was crumbling rapidly. Nick's every move was questioned. Every time he spoke, he was debated. As a result Nick became secretive, and before he spoke, he had to go through all of her possible debate scenarios in his head before he chose his words. He learned to perform this process instantly.

Nick dialed his home phone number. After four rings, Susan answered.

"Hello."

"Hey Susan. Listen. They want me to stay tonight to do transmitter proofs. Do you have a problem if I stay till 5:30? I will be home by 6."

"Like I give a shit. You're never here anyway. Your son is saying 'Daddy who?'"

Susan really knew how to push his buttons and seemed to enjoy doing it every chance she had.

"I really appreciate your support and understanding, honey. I'll just leave the bag of money on the kitchen table when I come in and I'll try not to bother you," Nick said sarcastically.

"Oh Nicky, while I have you on the phone, I want you to have someone work for you on the Fourth of July. Mom and Dad are having a get together at their house and I expect—"

Nick cut her off with, "Look Susan, I have to get back to work. I have a break coming up and this isn't the time or place to discuss this."

"Don't you dare hang up on me!" Susan said sharply.

"Does this sound like I'm hanging up on you?" Nick said as he slammed the receiver down in its cradle.

After a few cooling down minutes, he picked back up the receiver and dialed the transmitter number.

"Transmitter. Irv speakin'. It's your dime."

"Irv, Nick. I just got off the phone with my lovely bride and it's okay. I'll stay. Just send down some soda and chips. Sitting here looking at the waveform monitor and the multi-burst test signal on the air sure gives me the munchies, not to mention what your sparkling conversation does to me. As they say in the good old bluegrass state, 'It just don't get no better n'at.'"

"I'll call you about 15 minutes after sign off. Just take black and kill the carrier. I will fire it back up from here."

"Got it Irv. Later."

Nick switched the commercial break and took a well needed break himself. He went downstairs into the studio where the huge studio doors were opened wide. The heliport and parking lot were both in view, and the studio and scenic crews were setting up the kids' show for the following morning. Nick stepped outside into the hot and humid river town summer. He walked to the edge of the heliport, took a deep breath of heavy warm air and looked up to the full moon overhead. He wondered if this was as good as it was going to be for the rest of his life. Nick intertwined his fingers and placed his hands on top of his head. He slowly turned around and faced the studio. There was Lori in the studio, silhouetted by tens of thousands of watts of studio lights. She was holding a light meter and looking toward the lighting grid. Her long hair fell down her back, and he couldn't help but notice her young tight figure and full breasts. Her dress was made of a light summer weight material that allowed the light to come through and show off her perfectly shaped legs all the way up to the point where they came together. Maybe this wasn't as good as it was going to be for the rest of his life.

CHAPTER 7

Ten twenty and Nick had time enough to hie it back upstairs in time to catch the network mid break and set up the projection side of tele-cine for the 11:00 PM news. He took the stairs two steps at a time and made it to master control in time for the system's cue. The commercial break ended and all he could think of was how tired he was and why in the hell did he volunteer to stay all night. Nick found himself struggling often with the feeling that he didn't want to be at work so much but didn't want to be home either.

Nick returned to the projectionist's table to start preparing for the eleven o'clock news. He checked the program log and pulled the commercial slides that would have to be inserted correctly between the news slide segments. The commercial film reel was loaded on projector two, and he had switched control of the film and slide controls from MC to projection. It didn't take long until the news program director came up from the news room and brought the show rundown and news slides.

"Hey Nick," Sal, the director said. "The first and last slides need cleaning."

"From the look of these slides, it looks like someone had fried chicken down there while they were sorting these babies."

"Wrong choice, smart ass. Pizza," Sal replied. "With everything!"

Nick inserted the commercial slides in the proper sequence and loaded them into the slide drum leaving one slot empty on each side of the drum to mark where he started. He wrote the slot number next to the corresponding slide on the rundown. Frequently stories were killed or the order changed at the last minute and the projectionist had to locate and rearrange the slides on very short notice. It was 10:55, and the Technical Director in Control B called for control at MC. Nick went over to the master control switcher, waited for a pause in the dialogue, and took control B. There was often a jump in the audio when control was switched, since the audio levels may not have been exactly matched by the audio tech in the control room.

"You've got it in B," Nick called back over the intercom after the switch was made.

He made a slight audio adjustment then returned to the projection area. "Alan, give me control of video tape machines fifteen and seventeen, please."

"Will do. You should have it," Alan replied.

Just as Alan spoke, Nick noticed the red lights come on at the remote indicators. Everything was ready except for the news film. It was often late in coming upstairs, and tonight was no exception. As the news open was rolled at 11:00 straight up, Nick could hear someone running up the stairs with the news film reels. There were usually two reels, one main reel and one separate reel with reversals or cut-aways. As the film editor hit the top of the stairs, he tossed the main reel to Nick. Nick caught it and immediately began threading it on the projector. He could thread the projector in seventeen seconds. For the next half hour Nick rolled films, changed slides and rolled tapes as directed from the control room. He thought of Lori, who was operating a studio camera in the studio. Her shift was over at 11:30. Nick had about six hours to go. Just the thought of it depressed him.

CHAPTER 8

Eleven thirty finally arrived, and Nick took the network on the master control switcher.

"That's a good-night from control B," the TD called. "See ya tomorrow."

Nick settled in to watch the network late movie, when the hot line phone rang. "Master Control, Nick here."

"Nick, this is Irv. Gonna have to cancel tonight. Sorry, Bud."

"What happened, Irv? Got some soda in your finals?"

"Nah, I got to change out some tubes anyway. May as well do the proofs with new tubes. I should be ready, hopefully in a day or two, but you know how that goes. I'll let you know."

"No problem. I'd just as soon get the hell out of here anyway." Nick said with mixed feelings.

At 1:47am, after the religious program and sign off news, Nick took black and powered down the transmitter. He could hear Alan shut off the tape machines. There was a whoosh as the compressed air released from each machine. Nick always liked to just stand there and listen to the silence. You didn't realize how much noise the tape machines, equipment fans, and other miscellaneous machines made until they were all shut down.

"Hey Alan, ya hear that?"

"Nah, I don't hear anything."

"Yeah. That's what I mean. Nothing."

They smiled at each other and walked together past the night guard and to their cars in the parking lot. The air was heavy, and the smell of the bread baking at the bread factory across the interstate made him hungry. Within seconds he was on his way home. Nick turned on the radio and listened to some country music as his mind drifted to the silhouette of Lori. He smiled as he pictured her curled up in bed, peacefully sound asleep. He couldn't help but to fantasize that he was curled up with her, holding her tightly and synchronizing his breathing with hers. The glaring sound of a passing fire truck shocked him back to reality. His mind immediately switched to what he expected to find when he arrived home. There would be the usual sink full of dirty dishes, complete with the orts of supper, every surface of furniture and counter space covered with magazines, newspapers, clothing, or last week's junk mail. He envisioned Susan taking up most of the bed with the covers cocooned tightly around her with her back facing Nick's side of the bed, indifferent to whether he came home or not.

Even though they found it increasingly difficult sharing the same space at the same time, they still had occasional sex entirely for mutually selfish reasons. They both conceded that if it wasn't for love at least it felt good and relieved stress. The short fantasy about Lori had Nick a bit more than a little turned on. As Nick approached his exit on the interstate he thought, *wonder if she'd mind if I bothered her for a quickie before I crash. She can just call daddy and go to work late and besides, she can have plenty of time to rest up for the next one in a month or two.* Nick used to sadly joke to the guys at work, "Yeah, I asked her if she wanted to do it and she said 'Not this year, I have a headache.'"

At approximately 2:20 AM Nick pulled the Mustang into the driveway, turned off the engine and lights, and went up the steps to the front door of his "palace." He fumbled briefly with his bundle of keys, trying to identify the house key in the yellow glow of the front porch light.

CHAPTER 9

Nick turned the key in the lock and mumbled to himself, "Just another night in paradise."

He turned the doorknob and as the door swung opened he could see that the light in the foyer was on. The house was a split level, so he looked up the half flight of stairs and saw that the lights in the living room and kitchen were on as well. *What the hell is she still doing up at this hour?* he thought.

"Hey Susan, you still up?" he called.

There was no response, so he continued up the stairs to the first level. There was no sight of Susan. At the top of the stairs, Nick put his keys at their home on top of the fridge, turned right and proceeded to their son's room. The door was opened. Nick entered, as he did every night when he got home, to kiss his son on the forehead and tell him that he loved him. He walked to the bed and noticed that the blankets were mussed and there were some toys on the bed, but not his son. *What in the fuck is going on here?* he thought.

He felt the adrenaline rush overcome over him, and his heart began to pound hard in his chest. He could feel the tight feeling in his throat and his respiration quickened. The initial fear of foul play quickly passed and was replaced by the feeling that what was more likely was that Susan was doing some fooling around.

"I'll fix her ass." Nick said angrily.

He walked quickly and heavily back towards the stairs, grabbed his keys from the top of the fridge as he passed and went down the half flight of stairs and out to his car. Before getting into the Mustang, he stopped and looked through one of the six small garage door windows and saw that Susan's car was still parked there. He was getting increasingly pissed. Nick unlocked and opened his car door, got in and backed the car out to the street. His teeth were clenched so tightly that his jaws ached. Nick parked the Mustang around the corner, out of sight of the house so that Susan wouldn't know that he was home. Not giving a thought about the time or the fact that the rest of the neighborhood was asleep, he slammed the door shut so hard that he thought that the glass would break. Hurriedly he went back into the house and into his and Susan's bedroom, the room that used to be affectionately referred to during the early years of their relationship as the workshop. Without undressing he got into bed where he lied perfectly quiet and still. He could hear his heart beating loudly in his ears, and he could feel his pulse pound in his arms and legs.

After what seemed like hours, but in actuality was only about thirty minutes, he heard a key working in the front door and heard the door open as the wind guard attached to the bottom scraped against the floor tiles.

"Hey thanks," Nick heard Susan say. "I had a great time."

"Me too, babe," A twangy male voice said. "We gonna get together again some time soon?"

"I hope so. I'll have to let you know. Ya know, I don't get out too often, so this really felt good for a change."

The male voice said, "I gotta tell you, you're one ball of fire after you get a couple drinks down your neck."

"Speaking of ball," Susan said, "you ain't seen nothing yet."

"Just make sure that next time you wear those tight jeans again. By the way, did you spray them things on?"

"A girl's gotta keep a guy guessing, doesn't she?"

"Just don't make it too long before you call me, okay? I'll keep my engine running."

"Get out of here and go home. I'll call ya, I promise, and it won't be long...or is it?"

Nick heard them both laugh as the door shut. He could hear a car drive away at the same time he heard Susan's footsteps on the stairs. He could see the lights going off as she proceeded down the hall to the bedroom. Nick could see her form at the doorway as she felt around for the light switch and switched it on. Lori turned her head towards the bed and saw Nick.

"Jesus Christ, Nick. You scared the shit out of me. What the hell are you doing here? I thought you were at work."

Nick got out of the bed and stood six inches from Susan's face.

"That's pretty obvious. The question should be where the fuck have you been? And while we're playing twenty fucking questions, did you and Don fucking Juan have a good time playing with each other?"

"I didn't do anything wrong. I just went out for a few laughs with a couple of friends."

"And while you were out laughing your pants off, who is watching the baby?"

"He's fine. He's over at Paul and Beth's sleeping over with Todd. Why do you care if I go out? You're out till 2 a.m. a lot of the time."

"You bet your ass I am, except I'm out there working! You know, a job? Just something silly that I do to keep you in denim spray paint and beer. Jesus, Susan this isn't about me, it's about you fucking around on me. So, how many times have you and Mr. Smooth played hide the salami behind my back?"

"You sure are a paranoid shit, aren't ya?"

"So, I suppose that in happy little Susan world, your husband is married, but not you, right? Just get the fuck out of my face! I'm out'a here. Don't worry, I'll try not to get in your way while I decide what I need to do."

Nick stormed out of the room, slamming the door behind him so hard that the plaster cracked around the frame. He wanted to run as far as he could, but he was in a blind rage and felt trapped with nowhere to run. He went downstairs to the family room, where he had a small bar set up. He grabbed the first bottle in his reach, took it over to the sofa, and fell backwards into the large soft pillows. All he could think of was his wife being touched all over by another man and her giving herself totally to him, moaning with pleasure, her eyes rolled back in ecstasy. He felt his jaws tighten painfully again at the image. Nick removed the cap of the bottle and filled his mouth and gulping down the fiery liquid. He began to choke, but he kept it down. All he wanted to do was get shitfaced fast to make the pain and the images go away as soon as possible. Within minutes he could feel the numbness begin to come over his body. The second large gulp went down much easier.

It was as if a sheer curtain was being pulled across his vision and becoming a movie screen. The feature presentation starred him and Lori. Nick took another gulp and felt himself sink yet deeper into the pillows as his muscles, so tight with rage, began to let go. Nick's eyes closed. His mind's eye saw a peaceful white background with a vignette in the center containing him and Lori. They faced each other, holding on to each other's hands, looking longingly into each other's eyes. She was barefoot, wearing a light yellow peasant dress, her shoulder length hair blowing gently in the soft summer breeze. She had a lei of daisies around her neck. Nick released her hands and slowly, with his fingers slightly apart, slowly and sensually ran his fingers through her hair beginning just over her ears and catching her hair behind her neck with his thumbs. He lowered his thumbs and traced her neck and along her jaw line where they met beneath her chin. Lori slowly closed her eyes and tilted her head back as Nick placed a gentle kiss on that soft place between her jaw line and her neck, just below her right ear. Lori circled Nick's waist with her arms as his hands found her breasts. He could feel her begin to tremble. Lori met his lips with hers and almost immediately their lips parted enough for their tongues to find each other. They gently lay down on the soft grass.

The sound of the garage door opening and Susan's car starting in the garage not 20 feet from where he was sleeping rudely brought him back to the present. He could feel an ache in his temples and the dryness in his mouth, yet he found himself smiling. His eyes squinted and were out of focus, but he could manage to see the large red numbers of the digital clock across the room. It was seven thirty. His neck was stiff from the awkward position in which he slept. Another part of his anatomy was stiff as well. The bottle was overturned on the floor. Luckily or not, he had emptied it down his throat before it landed on the floor. Nick raised himself from the pillow nest and sat on the edge of the sofa with his head resting in his hands. After a couple of minutes he reached down to pick up the bottle. He felt very close to this dead soldier, as he was there when it passed away. With both hands he pushed himself up from the sofa to a standing position. He felt a bit dizzy. Nick wanted to go to bed, but he knew as soon as he hit the bed and smelled Susan's scent that it would bring it all back. Instead he opted to fix some coffee and just face the day. After all, he had seeing Lori at work to look forward to.

Nick showered, shaved, brushed his teeth, and poured a large to-go cup of coffee. He located his keys and went out to his Mustang that was still parked around the corner. Nick thought of the county park near where he lived. There was a quiet place where there was a stream, a covered bridge, and an old abandoned mill. It was there where he liked to go when he needed to be alone and "think." This was indeed the plan for the morning just as soon as the cobwebs cleared enough from his brain. Today, he had a lot to ponder; things that might well change the direction of his life.

CHAPTER 10

The Mustang seemed to be running on automatic as Nick headed down Hamilton Avenue, one of the main arteries through northern suburbia. Just a couple of miles south of the county line was a turn off to the right which wound its way along the bank of the stream, back to Nick's secret hideaway and special thinking place. He progressed through the first part of the "s" that was shaped by the stream, and it was here that he had his first glimpse of the corner of the old mill that once ground the grain from the farms just to the north. The mill was on the far side of the stream. There wasn't much left of the old mill except the three sides of the oxidized gray wooden structure which sat upon a five foot high foundation of field stone. If you looked very closely, you could still make out the original lettering of the old mill's name in old block letters on the side of the mill facing the lane. What was left of the wooden shingled roof was a patchwork of moss. The trees did a great job of keeping the area cool but also held the humidity in place. The covered bridge was just past the old mill and crossed the stream where the road split into a "Y."

Nick could hear the sound of the passenger side tires grinding the pea gravel edge of the lane as he pulled off on the berm just enough to allow other vehicles to pass. He shut off the engine and sat quietly for a moment. Although not consciously aware of it, Nick was holding his breath. He released it in a long sigh before opening the door. When he looked back down the road, he could see the cloud of gravel dust hovering above the road upon which he just traveled to get here. Nick closed and locked the door. He stood silently with his hands in his back pants pockets and stared into the canopy of the trees. The wonderful smell of the green from the grass and trees along with the muted sounds of the water washing over the rocks soothed his nerves.

He felt as if he were on an emotional carousel where each horse was a different emotion. The horse of anger would rise while the steed of self pity lowered. The ponies of hurt and sadness swapped positions while he was seated in the cart of abandonment. After Nick spun the wheel of misfortune a few turns in his head, he somewhat composed himself and walked down the bank to the water's edge. He followed the curve of the stream to where it flowed under the covered bridge. It was here that he found his flat "sitting rock" and settled in for a long and painful conversation with his inner self.

Nick leaned back on his elbows and stretched out his legs. He closed his eyes and lowered his head, which was still doing some temporal throbbing. *How could she do this to me? I try so goddamned hard to make things work and what do I get for it? What in the fuck am I doing? I just can't live like this. I don't want to leave my son, but I can't live this way either. Jesus! Why does it have to be so hard? No matter what I do it's never good enough for her. Yeah right, she's not doing anything with that asshole. Her ass probably has more fingerprints than the fucking FBI. I know I gotta get the fuck out of there, but where in the hell am I going to go? I can just live downstairs. Nah, I don't know. God, I can't even stand the sight of her anymore.*

After sitting on the rock for a while Nick's ass hurt almost as much as his head. He sat up, wrapped his arms around his shins and lowered his head to his knees. After a good old fashioned cry he decided that for now he would just have to suck it up and accept that it was just going get worse as time went on. One thing that he knew was that he had to do something to get his life in order. He wouldn't be any good for his son if he was always depressed and angry. He decided that he would better use this energy to do something positive for himself rather than create a thermal runaway situation of negativity. He would make a call to his attorney tomorrow and see where he stood and what his options would be. But for right now what he needed to do was to get his shit together and go to work. At least Lori would be there and just the sight of her would lift his spirits. Nick felt pretty badly about himself right now. He felt very lonely and like a total failure.

Nick thought out loud "Ain't I just the basket case. Why should I expect *any* woman to want to have anything to do with such a pitiful piece of work like me?"

He stood up, shook his head, and headed for the car. He was so wrapped up in his own pity party that he couldn't realize the spiritual hug that his stream and trees had given him.

CHAPTER 11

About eight weeks had passed since Nick had his life's critical moment. He had talked to an attorney and decided among other things that perhaps a change of scenery would be a good thing. One of his colleagues had within the last year taken a technical position at one of the networks. Nick thought, *What the hell, I'll give him a call and see if there are any openings coming up.* He had worked in the business long enough to have the confidence to go to one of the networks. Maybe Nick would call him in the morning.

Meanwhile, back at the "sausage factory" life goes on. The hot line in Master Control rang. "Master Control, Nick speaking."

"Nick-eee my man. This is Irv. Remember those proofs we talked about months ago? The rig is all re-tubed now and I'm ready to go. You with me?"

"When ya talking?" Nick asked, although he had nothing else to do, no matter when Irv wanted to do it.

"Actually, I know it's short notice, so if you want to do it tomorrow, it would be OK, but I'd really like to get it done tonight."

"That's cool. No problem. I'll be here. I'm off at 11:30 after the news, but I'll find something to do with myself till two thirty."

"Just don't go out and get too shit-faced to read those squiggly green lines on the scopes."

"Don't worry about me, Irv. Don't *you* get any soda in your finals."

Irv laughed his jolly old country laugh and said good-bye. Nick hung up and proceeded to get ready for the commercial break. While he was cleaning some commercial slides at the projection table, he noticed that Lori was helping at the video tape table. She was standing between the tape table and the video tape machines, facing his direction. Lori was leaning over slightly looking down at the program log and writing tape machine numbers next to the commercials. When her long hair fell down in front of her face, she flipped it back with a twist of her head. How badly he wanted to pull her hair back between his fingers. Lori raised her head and saw Nick looking at her. She smiled, as did Nick. He finished what he was doing and walked over to where she was working, a mere six or seven feet away.

"So, you sure are looking pretty comfortable with the job now."

"Just like you said I would be."

"It sure is good to know that someone thinks I know what I am doing around here. I can't always be wrong but I keep trying." Lori smiled.

"Maybe next year *you* can work with Irv doing the proofs."

"I suppose that by next year I will know more about reading scopes than just video, pedestal, and sync. Sure, why not?"

Nick couldn't imagine someone as beautiful as Lori having nothing better to do all night than babysitting a transmitter, staring into the dancing green image on the scope while having an old country boy whispering sweet technical somethings into her ear. He wished he were the something better to do.

"Well, I will be doing it tonight. Some fun, huh?"

"Isn't your shift over after the news? They have to wait till sign off to do the proofs, right?" Lori questioned.

"Yeah, but I'll find something constructive to do for a few hours in between." Nick said wearily. "Like take a nap."

Lori smiled and glanced down at the program log. With her head still tilted toward the video tape table Lori raised her eyes and said, "You better let me get the rest of this log marked before the news. I'm on probation, ya know?"

"You're right. I don't want to do something horrible like getting you fired." They both laughed and went back to what they were doing.

CHAPTER 12

"Eleven o-clock and time for the tri-state news." The audio cart announced over the opening news theme. Nick listened over the air monitor as his finger was poised on the roll button for the first headline film. Sal, the news director called for the roll of the film, and the news was on the way. Nick had done this drill so many times that he seemed to run on automatic. This was a good thing since his mind drifted from the stories of some poor souls who had lost everything in a fire or the fatal auto accidents to his own disastrous life.

After what seemed like an eternity, he was rolling the closing tape. Nick now had several hours of nothing to do to look forward to followed by an "Evening (more like morning) with Irvie." He signed off of the transmitter log and turned the Master Control over to his relief. Nick headed toward the maintenance shop to see if there was any coffee left worth drinking. As he turned the corner, he smelled the unmistakable smell of overcooked coffee on the verge of burning. He turned off the pot and proceeded toward the Chief's office across the hall. He just about reached the office door when he realized that he had left his jacket hanging on the back of his chair. He did a one-eighty back to the projectionist's table. When he got there, he noticed a folded piece of paper on the counter. Nick thought that he had thrown all of the papers away after the program. This wasn't trash, but a folded piece of paper with his name on it. "What the hell is this? I was just here 5 minutes ago, and there wasn't anything here." He pulled off the small piece of tape that held the note closed and unfolded it.

Nick, he read to himself, *I know you have a few hours before you need to do the proofs, and I thought that if you didn't mind driving a few miles you could come over to my place, and I could give you that thank you bev. I'll be up till about 1, so if you want to come over, here are the directions. Lori.*

The note contained detailed directions and a map. This was a dream, right? His heart was racing, and he could feel a flush come over his face.

CHAPTER 13

Nick couldn't get to his car fast enough. He took the stairs from tele-cine to the newsroom two at a time. Reaching the back door he pushed the door open nearly hitting an incoming news photog on his way back in from a live remote which had just aired a half hour earlier. He reached his car the same time he found the ignition key in his pocket. He couldn't seem to get the key into the ignition fast enough. As soon as the car started, he turned on the overhead light to look at the directions and map. The station was one block from the interstate, and Lori's exit was about six miles south, about 15 minutes drive this time of night. His fantasies were working overtime as he headed out of the lot abruptly stopping at the red traffic light nearly hitting a rather irate bread truck driver on a perpendicular course. "Jesus! I gotta get a grip here before I get killed." After regaining his composure, Nick proceeded more cautiously down the entrance ramp and onto the interstate.

Traffic was light, and Nick couldn't help but fantasize that Lori would be greeting him at the door dressed in a sheer teddy and holding a drink out to him. He imagined that she had the same feelings for him as he had for her. He forced himself back to the reality that the only thing that is, is what is. Lori simply invited him over for something to drink and a couple of hours of company to pass the time. That's all. He shook his head and smiled at the idiotic and pathetic way that his mind was playing with him. Lori's exit was coming up in about one mile. Nick turned on the overhead map light and with one hand unfolded the directions. *Take a left at the exit. Cross over the interstate and go to the second street on the left. There is a pizza place on the right. There are no lights, and the road is sort of winding, so be careful. When you reach a lake, about 1/2 mile, go around the right side. My place is in building 7, second floor, number 12. Park anywhere.*

That sounded easy enough. Lori's directions were perfect and in no time he was pulling into the parking lot of building 7 and into a visitor space right across from the entrance. Nick got out of the car and immediately noticed the peaceful quiet that was interrupted occasionally by the quacking of one of the pond ducks and a mating call of the indigenous frogs. There were several steps from the parking lot to the door which he took in one bounding leap. When he entered the hallway, he could smell the lingering aromatic mélange of this evening's dinners and the perfumes of the occupants. His heart pounded as he walked to the second floor and stood in front of apartment number 12. He could hear the sounds of country music coming from the other side of the door. *Well, here goes.* He thought to himself as he knocked on the door. After what seemed like an eternity but in reality was maybe ten seconds, he saw the doorknob turn and the door open.

"Hey, glad you decided to make it." Lori welcomed. "Come on in and make yourself comfortable."

"Thanks for inviting me. Sure beats the hell out of sitting around doing nothin' for three hours."

Nick was used to seeing Lori in business clothing, so the sight of her in tight Levi's, a loose fitting white oxford blouse, bare footed and her hair in a pony tail was surely a treat for his eyes. Nick felt overdressed since he was still in his work clothes, which was business attire, complete with tie.

"Kick off your shoes and loosen your shirt and tie. Make yourself at home. I'll get us a couple of beers, unless you'd like something stronger."

"As much as I'd like to, I don't want to pass out and make you have to carry me back to the station."

"You're right. We can't have you missing your date with Irv and getting arrested by the F.C.C." With that Lori turned and walked toward the kitchen. Nick settled into the armed wing chair while loosening his tie. What a great place Lori had. Although the living room lamps were on, there were aromatic candles burning on the end tables and a large round candle burning on the coffee table. There was a fireplace with the logs in position, just waiting for the perfect winter evening to warm the heart and home. Through the large glass door that opened onto a patio he could see a lighted geyser fountain in the middle of the lake. His thoughts were interrupted as he heard from the kitchen the distinctive hiss and pop of a beer bottle cap being propelled from its long necked launching pad.

"Ya want this in a glass?" Lori asked.

"Are you drinking yours from a glass?"

"Not me, I'm just a plain ole country girl."

"Well, I got so much class it's coming out my ass. Bottle is fine for me too."

Lori giggled as she popped the top off of the second bottle.

Nick loved the look and feel of her apartment. He wished he didn't have to go back to work.

Lori handed Nick a napkin and the beer bottle.

"Thanks. This is great."

"You're welcome. It's the least I could do after all the help and support that you have given me since I started."

Lori sat in the corner of the sofa where there were two large fluffy pillows. She tucked her right leg under her body and her left leg hung over the edge. *Damn, she's beautiful,* Nick thought. He held up his bottle in a salutary gesture and Lori did the same. They leaned toward each other until the bottle lips clinked as they gently touched. Nick wished badly that the lips touching were his and Lori's. Then they both took their first gulp at the same time.

"This sure hits the spot." Nick said as he wished for quite a different spot that he would like to hit right now. "So", Nick said with a slight sigh as he relaxed back into the chair, "now that we have some peace and quiet and about five less nosy people around, tell me all about yourself."

"There really isn't too much to tell. I got interested in show biz since my dad was on the radio. I used to hang around the studios a lot and got to know a lot of the country music folks. In high school we had our own little television station, and I started running one of the cameras for the morning homeroom report. Then I started doing some of the audio. I just really like the behind the scene stuff. I got my B.S. in radio and television, got my F.C.C first phone license and after I graduated I applied to all of the stations, but luckily, Malloy was the first to call and offer me a job. The rest is history. How about you?"

"Well, I started in high school where I was on the stage crew. I learned lighting and audio for the stage productions. In high school, my best friend who was a real techie, built a pirate radio station in his basement. I used to go over to his house and play DJ. A couple years after high school he went to broadcasting school for six weeks and landed a job at a small country station not far from right here. I used to hang out there, and the owner told me that if I got my first phone I could work there. I did, and soon I was making fifty dollars a week and all the records I could eat. I got married to my first wife, since she was with child, and after a few months of eating soup three times a day, I got my first job at a new UHF station in town. I got enough experience there to get a job at the station and now I'm living high. Impressed?"

"Actually, I am. First wife? How many have you had?"

"Do we have to talk about that right now?"

"I'm just curious, that's all."

"Ok, I am with my second wife right now, but I don't want to talk about it. It ain't pretty between us. As a matter of fact, I'm living in the basement family room right now. She has decided that while I am working nights she is going to be playing nights. Can we talk about something more pleasant, like maybe us having another brew? I'll fly if you buy."

"Sure, you shouldn't have too hard of a time finding the fridge. It's the large harvest gold box, that's yeller in Kentucky, next to the sink. Can't miss it."

Nick could tell that Lori was loosening up a bit. When he got up to get the beers, Lori reached behind her, turned off the lamp and stretched out her legs on the sofa. Nick brought the bottle to her. The small candle behind her was the perfect back light, and the candle on the coffee table gave her face a warm glow.

"Nick, is it getting a little warm in here or is it my imagination?"

"Yeah, it's getting a little warm in here, all right."

"Can you please slide the glass door open a bit and on the way back, how about turning the other lamp off, too, okay?"

Nick unlocked the door and slid it opened about six inches. He could hear the serene sounds of the crickets and the fountain. As he started back over to the wing chair Lori motioned him over to the sofa with a beckoning move of her index finger. As he approached the sofa, she patted the cushion showing him where to sit. There wasn't much room between her outstretched legs and the edge so he sat sort of side saddled on the sofa's edge with his left arm on the back of the sofa. He took a couple good chugs of the beer and set the bottle on the coffee table.

Lori smiled. "I think it would be all right for you to take the tie off and kick off your shoes. The boss isn't here."

She didn't have to say it twice. Nick removed his tie completely and kicked off his loafers. He turned back to Lori to see her unbuttoning the second button of her blouse. She pulled the blouse opened enough for Nick to see the tops of her breasts where they showed above her bra. Lori scooted back to a more upright position leaning against the arm of the sofa. For a moment, all Nick could do was to look into her eyes. He couldn't believe that he was here at all, let alone this close. He reached behind her head and unclipped the spring clip that was holding her hair together. Lori leaned forward and with both hands he loosened her hair from its previous shape and separated it so that it fell over her shoulder and down her back. Her hair was incredibly soft. Lori leaned back as Nick slowly leaned forward and placed his nose just below her left ear and touched her hair. He was immersed in that special fragrance that he loved so much. God, he could stay there all night. Lori put her hands on either side of his head and stroked his hair. Her chin was resting on his shoulder. Nick slowly pulled his head away from this Edenic place and looked longingly into Lori's eyes. Their eyes closed as their lips met. At first Nick just brushed his lips across hers, sort of a teasing gesture. Lori's lips were silky and soft, and he pressed against them harder. Slowly their mouths opened enough to let their tongues meet. Nick gently pulled away and placed his mouth right at the point where her breasts met and gave her a kiss. Lori lightly bit her lower lip and inhaled making sort of a reversed F sound. She slowly scooted down to where her head was resting on the arm of the sofa. Nick spread his fingers through her hair and slowly moved his fingertips down the sides of her neck, over her shoulders and down to her chest where they barely touched her breasts and found their way to the buttons that were still fastened. She tilted her head back more and arched her back so that her breasts raised to meet him. Her nipples hardened, and he could clearly see their outline through her bra and blouse. Nick nervously unbuttoned the remaining buttons, opened her blouse and revealed what he had longed to see. Lori leaned forward and reached behind and under her blouse to unfasten her bra. Nick lifted the bra over the top of her breasts to expose them. He quickly covered them with his hands and kissed her on the mouth. Her nipples were quite hard, and he couldn't wait to feel them between his lips.

Lori slightly spread her legs, and Nick knelt between them. He slowly ran his tongue from her lips, down her chin then skipped to her breasts. He circled each nipple and gave each a gentle tug with his lips. His tongue traced a line from between her breasts down to her navel. Lori's skin was covered with goose bumps, and she began to move her hips. Nick unbuttoned her jeans and unzipped them. Her bikinis were cut low enough to let about one half inch of her pubic hair exposed. He was about ready to explode. Lori reached down and with a hand on either side of his head, gently and slowly raised Nick's head up to where his chin rested on her chest and his eyes looked up to meet hers. Nick noticed tears forming in her eyes, and she had an apologetic look on her face. No words were spoken as Nick righted himself back into a sitting position and awkwardly resituated his anatomy to a less painful position. At the same time, Lori slid down enough to flatten out her back so that she could zip up her jeans. Nick watched as she slowly removed her bra the rest of the way and buttoned up her blouse. The gates of Eden were now closed, and he was looking through it from the outside. Neither Nick nor Lori could find a word to say. The atmosphere in the room was getting thicker by the minute. Looking at her became increasingly more difficult. His eyes drifted to his watch which read *1:47* AM. He couldn't believe that the time had flown so quickly. He had to get back to the station. He didn't want to go, yet he didn't want to stay either.

"Lori, I have to get going. Irv'll shit a preverbal brick if I'm not there right at sign off. I really appreciate your having me over tonight. Maybe we can get together again…soon?"

"Glad you accepted my invite. Guess I'll see you at the old grind tomorrow. Drive carefully."

"Will do." Nick replied as he stood up, did a final re-arrange of himself, and headed for the door with Lori following. Nick was really confused as to what had just happened, or more like what didn't happen, so he resisted the urge to give her a goodbye kiss. He just half smiled, nodded his head toward her, and took a final look at the scene of the crime before turning and walking away. As he walked away, he could hear the door close behind him. Nick was experiencing a cerebral tornado of feelings right now. The last thing he wanted to do was to go back to work and face hours of mind numbing proof of performance readings with Irv. There was no way he would be able to concentrate on what he was doing, and he was expected to be exacting of the readings. He didn't want to go to his emotionally void and un-welcoming cold home, and he felt that he was just ejected from the garden. Unfortunately, he really didn't have a choice. Nick had to go back to work and muddle through as best as he could, then go home and hope for a better day. As for Lori, well, he'd just have to wait until tomorrow and see what it would bring.

CHAPTER 14

4:30 AM. Nick and Irv finished up earlier than expected. Almost all off the readings were within legal parameters, and therefore few adjustments needed to be made. Between the mind numbing proofs and emotional and physical exhaustion, Nick delayed the beginning of his solo pity party until a later time. Right now, as cold and unwelcoming as his home was, it was a familiar place to crash, so it was in that direction the Mustang was aimed.

Nick pulled the Mustang into the driveway around 5:00 AM. It was still dark as he secured the car and walked the half flight of concrete steps to his front door. In the few seconds that it took to separate out the house key from the rest on the key ring, a years worth of flashbacks and emotions, ending with the evening with Lori, went through his mind. As soon as the door opened, he went into automatic mode, tossing his keys on top of the fridge as he passed the kitchen, then heading down stairs to "his" room. He wondered if Susan was even home but was too tired and worn out to really give a shit. All he really wanted to do was get a super-sized shot of Jack down his pie hole and try to travel to La La Land before the sun poked up over the horizon.

After what seemed like seconds, but in fact was a couple of hours, he woke to the sound of water running through the pipes as Susan was taking her shower. He lied there restlessly until he heard her leave the house for the day, thereby knowing that at least for the time being he would be left the fuck alone.

"C'mon boy, Mommie's running late. Where's your back pack?"
"I want to say goodbye to Daddy."
"Just get in the car. You can see Daddy later. Let's move it!"

Susan seemed to have as much patience for her son these days as she did for Nick.

The door slammed shut, and the sound of the engine starting signaled the start of the next couple of hours of sleep. The quiet was almost deafening.

CHAPTER 15

The day started out beautifully, as far as the weather was concerned, but rapidly deteriorated into gray and dismal, pretty much the way that Nick was feeling at the moment. He had to get the hell out of his nightmare, but what would become of his son if he left, being raised by The Bitch. What will he say to Lori when he sees her this afternoon? What will she say to him? He didn't have any more time to sit and worry about it. It was time to get his shit together, both inside and out, and head for work. Work was the only constant in his life right now, the only thing that he could count on to be there when he arrived.

By the time that Nick got to the car, it had started raining and there were rumbles of thunder echoing from distant hills. Although he grabbed his umbrella as he exited the door, it wasn't needed for the five yard dash to the car. Since he had presence of mind to at least have the car key at the ready, his entrance into the vehicle occurred with only minor dampness to his person. Having tossed the umbrella onto the passenger seat, Nick started the car, shifted into reverse and backed out of the driveway and into is day.

After a somewhat longer than usual commute to work, he pulled into the employee parking lot and into one of the ten spaces assigned to engineering. Even with the delay due to the weather, he was still ten minutes early for his shift. It was raining harder now, so the umbrella was deployed immediately upon exiting the Mustang. As he walked down the row of cars, just past the heliport, he noticed that Lori had already arrived.

"Aw shit." Nick said aloud but to himself, "Here goes nothing. Oh well, it's show time!"

He continued the "last mile" to the employee entrance, and once under the shelter of the overhang, he vigorously "pumped" the umbrella open and closed to jettison as much water as he could before entering the building. Just on the other side of the glass air lock sat the headset clad switchboard operator whom although in the middle of a call, "buzzed" Nick in and took the time to smile and do the wave with her fingers as he pushed open the heavy glass door. After returning the gesture and mustering up a smile as best he could, Nick proceeded up the stairs to tele-cine. An immediate left after Malloy's office and Nick was there. Lori was about ten feet away, standing at the video tape table facing away from where he entered. Sensing a presence, she turned and upon seeing Nick gave him a smile so warm that it immediately melted the icy chill of his anxieties. They each took a few steps toward each other, closing the distance between them to maybe eighteen inches.

"Hi Nick, how ya doin'?" Lori asked in her pert country voice.

Nick lowered his eyebrows a bit, as if he didn't quite get what she was saying. "Ok," was all he could say, as it came out like a question. He then added, "I really had a good time last night. Thanks for the southern hospitality. How about you?"

"Me too. Glad you took me up on the offer."

Now more composed and relaxed, Nick produced enough fortitude to ask, "So, do ya think we can get together again?"

"Maybe. We'll see." She replied in a more serious tone.

Not very encouraging, but enough for Nick to venture out a "Soon?"

Lori, feeling a little uncomfortable with the tone of urgency on Nick's part, could only reply, "I said, we'll see."

Nick wasn't quite sure just where his head was at any one time these days, but he was together enough to know that this one had to be let go for at least a while.

"Got it." Nick said, as he turned and slowly walked over to the daily duty schedule to see where he was assigned for the remainder of this long day.

CHAPTER 16

Seasons passed and although the joyous sights, sounds and smells of the holiday season had arrived, Nick's senses were numb to them all. It had become increasingly clear to him that changes had to be made and soon. The only thing that changed in the past six months was that he no longer slept downstairs. He moved back into his and Susan's bedroom, but she insisted on a hands off policy. The romantic feelings had long gone, but Nick still found her to be extremely attractive and longed for the touch of her soft skin and the feel of her hair as it lightly caressed him. He couldn't help but vividly remember the electric excitement that passed through him whenever they touched. Now, the best that he could hope for was to wait until she was asleep and slide himself over to her so that his back lightly touched hers, recall past love making and do what he had to do while trying not to wake her.

Nick was in the middle of one of these fantasy sessions when Susan awoke.

She sat up startled and said curtly, "What in the hell are you doing?" She glanced over at the clock on the night stand, turned back to Nick and added, "For Christ's sake it's two AM!"

Nick, now frustrated and a little bit embarrassed replied, "Nothing that you would be interested in, at least not with me. Hold it down before you wake the baby."

"What in the fuck do you mean by that?!"

"What do you mean, 'what do you mean?' You know exactly what I mean, and keep your voice down. The neighbors don't need a midnight matinee. If you're really that dense that you can't figure out what I'm talking about, let's try it like this. Susan is out with Macho Man cowboy playing hide the salami while Nicky baby works his ass off trying to keep food on the table and a roof over your head. The cowboy gets the kitty, and Nicky gets to date the five ladies. Is that as clear as shit for ya?"

"What am I supposed to do, become a nun since you are never here? I'm sick of sitting around here by myself every evening, spending holidays with everyone but you. What do you expect me to do? Am I supposed to amuse myself on the weekends by darning socks, churning butter, going to quilting bees, and baking toll house fucking cookies! If that's what you want from a woman, then go find an Amish chick. I'm sick of it, Nick. Goddamn sick of it!" By this time the tears were pouring from Susan's eyes, and she held her face in her hands and sobbed. She reached for the box of tissues, but Nick had put them on his side of the bed in preparation for his evening's date with the five ladies. He grabbed a handful of tissues and handed it to Susan. "Here."

Susan looked up at Nick, took the tissues, and wiped her red eyes and nose.

"Susan, you knew what kind of work I did and what the schedule was like before we got married. Now, all of a sudden it's a big bad surprise? Bullshit! You always say and do what you have to to get what you want, then you aren't satisfied and want more. Yeah, I work a lot of overtime. What's here to make me run home after work, the arms of a loving wife? Shit, Susan, I have some needs too. I have physical needs as well as the need to know what in the hell I'm going to be doing from now on. I know one thing for sure, I can't go on like this."

"I'm not going to get into a pissing match with you about the loving wife shit, but did you forget that you have a son to hurry home to? You're wrapped so tight in your own shit, I'll bet you don't even know when his birthday is, let alone that he even exists."

That salvo hit right to the heart. Nick loved his son very much but knew that as much as he would like to leave with him, it was impossible. The father never gets custody of the children, unless the mother is a convicted chain saw murderess. He also knew that he couldn't stand living like this for another fourteen years, until his son reached eighteen years of age.

"June eighth." Nick said.

"What?"

"June eighth, our son's birthday. You said I didn't know when his birthday was."

"Jesus, Nick, I can't take this shit any more. I'm moving into the baby's room." With that she grabbed her pillow, pulled the blanket off of the bed and dragged it down the hall to the other room. At least she didn't literally slam the door, although a door most definitely had slammed shut. It was at this time that Nick knew exactly what he had to do, and do it soon.

CHAPTER 17

It was Saturday evening, and Nick had just finished video switching the six PM news and the network news was on air. As he was rising from the Technical Director's chair, he noticed a familiar face at the control room door. It was his friend Larry, a colleague who had left the station a year ago to take a TV technical job at the Global News Network in Washington, DC. G.N.N. was gearing up to begin broadcasting television worldwide. The parent company was broadcasting radio and television programs nationwide over affiliated stations, but now the new G.N.N. was planning to start airing programs targeted to specific regions worldwide via satellite.

"Larry, what the hell brings you back here?"

Larry entered the control room and reached for a handshake. "I have a week off for the holiday and thought I'd stop by and see what's happening. So, how ya been?"

"Sorry you asked. Actually, things are going okay, I guess. Must be nice to have a holiday off."

"Actually, it is. I get to play TV but without the pressures of commercial TV. Have every holiday off, work eight to four forty five and weekends off. Like a real life, I really love it. So, what's new here? Lori still here or did the fossils drive her off with their 'get the broads out of broadcasting' shit?"

Nick replied, "Not only did they not drive her off, but there are two more."

A big teeth baring grin appeared on Larry's face. "Well, ain't that some shit."

Nick could only smile back while thinking to himself, "If you only knew."

"So, while you're here, you planning on comin' to the Christmas party?"

"Wouldn't miss it. We are really gearing up programming in D.C., so this may be the last one that we'll be able to come to."

The station really had some great Christmas parties that were held in the largest of the studios, studio "A." It was held in the studio so that the personnel that were on duty that day could steal away a few minutes between tasks and come down and participate. There was a great catered buffet dinner, music by a dance band led by the station's own announcer, Herman, family photos taken by the staff photographer, and of course there was Santa with a large bag full of gifts especially chosen for each employee's child. Santa was played by one of the station's rather rotund and vocally gifted technicians, Henry. Henry, rather, Santa was equipped with a small earpiece connected to a walkie-talkie cleverly hidden beneath his hat. At the other end was one of the child's parents secretly feeding information to Santa, like his or her name, age, pet's name, etc. This never ceased to amaze the kids. Watching the kids' reactions was one of the high points of the party, and for Henry too, who at age 60 was never married and loved children.

CHAPTER 18

Just outside of the studio, in the visitor's lobby, was the family photo area. "Next" called Ben, the station's staff photographer and film department editor.

"That would be us, I guess," answered Nick, as he placed his hand on his son, Adam's shoulder and gently steered him to the lighted area. Susan followed. Nick gently lifted Adam and sat him on one of the large yellow prop cubes facing the camera. Susan stood next to Adam at the camera left position and Nick to the right. Adam looked so great. His blonde, curly hair was a little over his collar. He was wearing a white shirt and little blue sweater vest. This was *his* day and his smile and antsy eagerness to get back to the party were clear signs. The host of the children's program was putting on a show for the employee children, and Adam didn't want to miss out on one second. Susan was dressed in what Nick felt was an inappropriately too tight and too low cut long, black dress and boots. Her hair fell to the middle of her back.

"Smile!" bellowed Ben's voice from behind the camera, as this family moment was captured in time. A smile seemed to come effortlessly to Susan and Adam but was a difficult task for Nick. This was supposed to be a happy time which made Nick feel even more emotionally conflicted. At Ben's cue, "Next!" Nick lifted Adam from the cube and placed him gently down. He immediately ran back into the studio to the show. Nick and Susan followed and went back to the table which they shared with Larry, his wife and two kids, and one other family.

Susan took her seat and as Nick was about one third into his, Susan asked, "So, Nicky, how about buying your wife a drink?"

As close as he could answer without appearing angry or sarcastic, he answered, "Sure, what'll it be?" while at the same time thinking *hemlock and soda?*

"I think I'd like a glass of wine." Susan answered.

The first thing that came into Nick's mind was *Let's see…what goes best with asshole…*then aloud, "Red or white?"

"White," she decided, "and can you add a splash of soda? I just love the bubbles." This immediately replayed in his mind an earlier time in their lives when champagne played a non-traditional part in one of their more playful moments, and how she and her cowboy might be enjoying that right now. He felt his face turning red with impending rage as he turned to go to the beverage bar. On his way past the buffet table, he noticed Lori sitting at a table across the studio. Nick recognized all but one of the people at her table. The one that he didn't recognize had his left arm around her shoulder and holding her rather closely. That was all he needed to see right now. All he wanted to do right now was to go home and lose himself with his friend, Jose' Cuervo. As this was not a viable alternative at the moment, he proceeded to the beverage bar were he met Alan who was nursing a can of beer and listening to Herman and the boys play the oldies.

"Ya havin' a good time, Nick?" Alan almost yelled to be heard over the music.

"Oh sure. We're sitting over there with Larry and family. C'mon over and liven things up."

"Nah, looks like Susan is doing a good enough job of entertaining your table over there. The best show is from here, at least as long as the hooch supply holds up. What'll ya have, pardner?"

"I need something stronger than what they have here, but I'll settle for a couple beers before I go back to the table. You have any idea who that is over there with Lori?"

"Uh, uh. All I know is that she got out of a car with Florida plates with that dude. Want me to do some re-con for ya?"

"No, I'll find out." Nick's eyes kept traveling between watching Susan which pissed him off and to Lori and her dude which made him feel jealous. *Why should I feel jealous,* he thought, *It's not like we have something going. Maybe it's just the thought of any couple in love that's doing it.*

"I better get back to the table with Susan's wine before she really makes a scene with me. She's already over there sending daggers at me with her eyes. I'll see ya tomorrow." Nick got the bartender's attention and ordered Susan's white wine with a splash. As the bartender handed the glass to Nick, Alan lifted his beer can as if to toast and gave a nod adieu. Before heading to the table, Nick gave one more look towards Lori's table. At the same moment she looked his way and their eyes met. He felt a pang in his chest as he turned away and went back to his reality.

"That sure took long enough." Susan said as Nick handed her the glass. "I'm so thirsty I might have to send you back for another one right now." There wasn't going to be another one as far as he was concerned, and as soon as Santa finished giving out the gifts, he was planning on going home.

"Larry, I'd like to have a sit down with you before you leave. Do you have plans tomorrow afternoon?"

"How 'bout we meet at Skyline for lunch. I sure could use a chili fix before I head back. 12:30 ok?"

"I'll be there."

Just then, Lori's rising from her chair caught his eye. She was as beautiful as ever. He had seen her in her "work" clothes but never so beautifully dressed. She was wearing a white mini dress with ¾ length sleeves. Her bare shoulders were covered with a red shawl over which her beautiful long hair fell. She was wearing calf high boots. The one thing that he didn't like that she was wearing was that guy on her side. Lori and her date passed within feet from where he was sitting to get to the studio door. Nick couldn't help but to observe her exit.

"Whoa big fella." Susan said, "You darned near got whiplash there!"

Nick didn't realize how obvious he had been. Everyone at the table laughed except Nick. After about one half hour, Santa's job was finished, and the party was winding down. Nick's mind was on vacation during that time, something that seemed to happen with more frequency these days. He went over to where Adam was playing with some of the other kids and told him that it was time to go home. After gathering up Adam, his new toy truck, and Adam's napkin full of cookies for the road, they went to the table to get Susan. Susan was pretty well lit by this time and resisted the idea that the party was over. As far as Nick was concerned, the party was over in more ways than one. She finally relented, and they headed for their coats. He helped Adam with his coat and handed Susan hers.

"Aren't you gonna be a gemmeman and help me put this on?" she loudly slurred.

Since this clearly drew attention, he gritted his teeth and held the coat while she slipped her arms into it. He couldn't wait to get to the car and get out of there.

It was cold and dark when they reached the Mustang in the parking lot. His gloved hands fumbled with the keys. He opened the passenger side door and released the front seat back so that Adam could crawl into the back seat. After Adam was buckled in, Nick pulled the seat back up to the latched position and poured Susan in. Shortly they were all inside, buckled in, and on their way home. Adam quickly fell asleep holding his new truck. Susan sat there swaying here head from side to side to the beat of the music from the radio.

The only words spoken during the whole trip were Susan's, "I gotta pee."

CHAPTER 19

Nick made the final turn into the driveway and shut off the engine. Both car doors opened at the same time. Susan didn't even close her door as she literally ran up the steps. She unlocked the door and without even closing it behind her, headed straight for the bathroom. Nick unbuckled Adam, who was only half awake, picked up his cookies and truck and headed for the door. Since his arms were full, he used his foot to push the car doors closed. By the time they reached the living room, Adam was fully awake. He dropped his coat on the floor and took his booty to his room to play.

"Please change into your play clothes. Before you play, ok?" Nick asked.

The only reply was "K."

Nick placed his keys on top of the fridge and headed for his room downstairs and his rendezvous with Jose'. He changed into his blue jeans and sweatshirt, and collected the good Mr. Cuervo and a glass from the other side of the room. He turned on the stereo as he passed and fell into his overstuffed chair ass first, feet to follow. Susan could be heard upstairs as she walked on the uncarpeted floor of the kitchen overhead. Nick opened the bottle and released his Mexican genie into the glass. He knew that after a short while his genie would be granting him his wish of emotional numbness and a ticket to dreamland. The first shot was a quick one designed to kick start the process, followed by the second, and then less frequent shots to maintain the buzz. He didn't know if it was his imagination or not, but Susan's footsteps seemed to be getting louder and closer. He wasn't imagining it. In a matter of seconds, there she was, standing right in front of his chair. How different she looked from just an hour ago. Hair in a ponytail, tight white t-shirt which clearly showed the world that it was cold, and her spray on jeans. As much as he hated it, with all of the fighting and anger between them, she still stirred something within him, even if it was just a physical reaction.

"So, what was that all about?" Susan interrogated.

"What was what all about? What the hell are you talking about?" She did this a lot to him. For no apparent reason, just come up with something out of the blue to argue about.

"You know what I'm talking about. You couldn't take your eyes off of that chick at the party. So, you have a thing for teenagers now?"

"First of all, she's not a teenager. She's a tech."

"Bullshit. She's more like the staff hooker, dressed in those 'come fuck me' clothes and boots."

"Are you still drunk or are you just plain bat shit? What are you talking about anyway? Don't you look in the mirror when you get dressed?"

"There isn't a damn thing wrong with the way I dress."

"Jesus, Susan, I'm not even going to talk to you about this. I refuse to get into a battle of wits with an unarmed person."

"Screw you! I'm outta here. I'm going out with some friends. Don't wait up."

Susan ran up the stairs cursing under her breath.

"I'll tell Adam that Mommy says goodnight. If he asks where you are, I'll tell him that you're out having a rodeo with your very own cowboy. Better call your cowboy and tell him not to forget his rope and his goat."

At this point, it was probably a good thing that Nick was in the company of his closest amigo, Jose', because he had nearly reached the breaking point. His felt as if each one of his arms had a ten pound weight attached as he reached for the bottle. "One last kiss goodnight." He said to the bottle as he raised it up to his lips. There was just enough for maybe one half shot, just enough to send him off to dreamland. The last sound that he remembered hearing as the curtain was coming down, was the slamming of the front door.

The sound of breaking glass caused him to spring to an upright position. His heart was pounding and the cranial cobwebs were thick as he pushed himself out of the chair to a standing position. He was standing still, while the room spun around him. After a few moments, Nick made his way up the stairs, where at the top he could see into the kitchen.

"Jesus Christ! What happened?" he queried Adam who was standing barefoot amid the shattered remains of a large glass bowl, holding a one half gallon carton of milk cradled in his arms as if it were his teddy bear.

Adam had tears in his eyes as he explained, "Mommy went away, and I was hungry. I was getting some Captain Crunch."

"It's all right, sweetie. Don't move and Daddy will clean up the glass so you don't cut your feet."

With that he took the milk from Adam's grasp, bent down and lifted Adam from the floor. Nick could feel his heart beat strongly in his head as he brushed off Adam's feet and sat him down on the sofa in the living room while he swept up the floor. He fixed Adam a bowl of cereal and sat with him on the sofa until he finished. Normally, Adam wasn't allowed to eat in the living room, but right now it just didn't matter. He watched his son intently as his little mouth crunched the cereal, spoonful after overfull spoonful. He knew what he needed to do. He felt as if he were a stranger in his own home and his fantasy of ever hooking up with Lori was shattered just hours ago. Nick felt an emptiness in his chest. He tried to imagine what life would be like without having Adam around, if he left. God, he loved his son more than anything. He had no idea where to turn or what to do. He was meeting with Larry tomorrow. Maybe things would look differently in the morning. Hopefully for the better.

"C'mon son. Let's go to bed." Nick took the bowl from Adam's lap and placed it on the coffee table. He lifted Adam and looked into his eyes. "Ya know that Daddy loves you big, don't you?"

"I love you big, too." Adam responded.

"How'd you like to come and snuggy with me downstairs?"

Adam smiled and nodded. Nick carried Adam down the stairs and sat him on the couch.

"Read you a story?" Nick had one arm around Adam's shoulder, holding him close. His silky blonde hair smelled like baby shampoo. This was going to be the toughest decision of his life...maybe.

Before long, they were both lying on the sofa asleep, curled up together. How many more opportunities like this would there be?

CHAPTER 20

Nick woke up first. His right arm was numb as he slowly pulled it from beneath Adam's head. He climbed over Adam and went into the bathroom. He was incredibly thirsty and drank from the cup formed by his two hands held closely together and filled from the bathroom sink tap. Nick checked the time. It was 7:30 AM. He could hear the water running upstairs as Susan showered for work. Nick went upstairs to retrieve the paper from the driveway. There it was, just behind Susan's left rear tire. There was a tire mark on the paper that matched the tire of her car. You didn't have to be Sherlock Holmes to figure out that Susan was out all night. Nick often caught sight of the delivery around 4:30 AM, right before he left for work.

"Who really gives a shit at this point." He muttered to himself as he picked up the paper and went back inside.

Adam had awakened by this time and was eating a piece of toast while Susan was gathering up her purse and coat. She bumped Nick as she passed and headed for the door.

Nick remarked "Nice bumping into you this morning. Have a great frickin' day" and continued under his breath "bitch." Susan didn't hear the last word as the door slammed at the same time.

Nick poured himself a cup of coffee and took it with him to the bathroom where he showered and shaved. Upon completion of his morning rituals, which included working the crossword puzzle, he asked Adam, "Adam, Daddy needs to go out for a while. Would you like to go over to Pat's for a visit if it's OK with her?" Pat was an elderly lady who lived across the street. She had two young dogs that Adam loved to play with.

"OK. Can I take my new truck and show her?"

"I'll ask her." Nick dialed Pat's number and after two rings she answered.

"Hello."

"Hi, Pat, this is Nick from across the street. Susan is working, and I need to go out for about two hours. Can you watch Adam and his truck for me?"

"No problem. Would be happy to. What time will you be coming over?"

"About 11 ish?"

"Sure. See you then."

After dropping off Adam and his truck, Nick headed for the Skyline to meet Larry. Upon arrival he noticed that Larry was already there and sitting in a booth where he had a view of the door. As soon as he opened the door, he could feel the warm, moist and heavenly scented air of the specialty of the house, Mediterranean style chili.

Nick reached the booth where Larry sat and reached out to shake his hand. "Good to see ya, Larry."

"Me too, let's order and talk while we eat. I'm starving."

"Sounds like a winner to me."

Almost immediately the waitress came over. "What'll it be boys?"

"I'll have a three-way, two cheese conies with onions and mustard, and a soda."

"Ditto for me." Nick echoed.

A three way is an oval plate lined with spaghetti, topped by a rather runny and finely textured aromatic chili mixture of Greek origin, finely chopped onion on top of that, and then smothered with finely grated yellow cheese. This is usually served with a side of oyster crackers and hot sauce to kick it up. The conies are simply hotdogs on buns, mustard, chili mixture poured over the hotdogs and topped with cheese. This is a very regional dish and is rarely found outside of the area.

The first thing to arrive at the table were the bowls of oyster crackers.

"So, Nick, I told you what's up with me yesterday. What's up with you?"

"Well, it's no secret that Susan and I aren't hitting it off too well these days. I really need a change in my life."

"I figured as much. You could cut the tension with a knife between you two yesterday."

"I know. Bottom line is that she has too much time alone. I mean, she has Adam there but not me. You know the schedules that we have. Working lots of nights and weekends, and almost every holiday, unless it's our day off. Well, she seems to have found her adult entertainment elsewhere."

"That's why I left and came to work for G.N.N. I got tired of having no life."

The plates of food were placed on the table in front of them and the aroma made Nick's mouth start to water. "Can we have some more crackers?" he asked the waitress. Both Nick and Larry had dispatched the first order of crackers while talking.

"Sure, hon. Bring 'em right over."

"So, Larry, how do I get a piece of that?"

"I'll send you the application. Fill it out and send it back to me and I will hand deliver it to personnel. If they are interested, you will get a security packet to fill out. Give it a try and see where it goes. What ya got to lose?"

"Nothing, I guess. I have a four day weekend coming up. How about I come out to D.C. and check the place out?"

"Sounds great. You can stay at our place."

Nick felt better already. There just may be some light at the end of the tunnel. A new job, a new city, a new life. Sounded pretty good. "It's a deal. I'll start working on it right away."

Nick sprinkled some hot sauce on the pile, cut a one inch chunk and lifted it to his mouth. *If heaven had a flavor, this had to be it*, he thought. After some idle chit chat about life's issues in general, Nick and his overstuffed but very happy tummy said good-bye and headed home. What a difference a day makes, just knowing that there are possibilities out there. He knew that nothing was a sure thing, but as one can learn from the turtle, if you don't stick your neck out, you will never get anywhere.

CHAPTER 21

Nick returned to work following his two days off and upon entering tele-cine he saw Lori. She was standing on a chair and reaching on her tip toes to place a video tape box on the second shelf. As she reached, her mini-skirt inched higher and higher. It was like passing a car wreck. It was painful to look at, but you couldn't turn away.

Alan's "Eh, yo" from behind startled him back to the real world. "Pretty fun Sunday, huh?"

"Yeah, for who? Looked like Lori was havin' a pretty good time. Find anything out about her secret life?"

"Just that he was some dude that she was pretty hot after in high school. He got some college deal in Halitosis, I mean Tallahassee. He went away to school, she didn't, he's done, and he's back. You'll have to get the mi-noots from her."

"Thanks, Kojak. You've been a great help."

"Always eager to help. Can't wait till my next assignment."

"Don't you have a real job? Try doing it."

Nick signed in and went over to where Lori was working. "Have fun at the party? I would have come by and chatted with you, but it looked like you were pre-occupied. You think we could get together, just me and you some evening after work and chat?"

"Nick, I told you, I don't want to feel pressured, especially right now."

"Well, how about we just meet in the break room before you leave today? I'll only keep you for a few minutes, and I promise, no pressure. I just have a few things that I need to get straight in my mind to help me decide what I need to do."

"All right. I'm off at two thirty."

"I'll meet you there right after I do the two thirty break."

It seemed like forever to their meeting. Immediately after the break Nick ran downstairs to the break room. As promised, there was

Lori sitting at one of the futuristic looking white plastic café tables. As he passed her to go around to the other side of the table, he got a good look at her beautiful legs. She noticed his eyes fondling her legs, so she took her coat and laid it across her lap. He pulled out the chair across from her, sat, and looked into her eyes.

"Lori, ever since we were together at your place, you have pretended that nothing happened that night. It was very special for me, even though we didn't do anything. I can't get it out of my mind, and you act like it never happened. Didn't it mean anything to you? Remember, it was you that invited me over."

"Nick, you promised no pressure."

"I'm not trying to pressure you. I just can't figure it out. Can you just tell me what happened and why you refuse to even acknowledge that something happened that night?"

"Is this all that you want to talk about? If so, I have a lot of things to do right now so I have to go."

"I'm sorry, I just have a lot of things going on in my life right now, and it is getting very complicated and confusing."

"Do you think that I don't have any issues to deal with? That I just come to work, go home, read a book, go to bed, repeat if necessary? Our ships passed and they bumped. Life goes on."

Nick realized that this road was going nowhere, so he changed directions. The alternative route was destined to be a bumpy one also, but what the hell.

"Lori, I was talking to Larry at the party, and there may be an opportunity for me to change jobs and move to D.C. You are the first one that I have talked to about this. I feel like I need to bounce this off of someone, and I'd like it to be you."

"Shouldn't you be talking this over with your family first?"

"I can't talk to Susan about this right now. All she will do is blow up. Besides, if I decide to do this, she won't be moving with me."

"Ouch!" Lori winced. "I didn't realize that things were so bad at the home front. I guess you gotta do what you feel is right."

"I can't stay in this relationship and live like this anymore. The biggest problem is having to leave my son, but it can't be good for him to be living in such a hostile environment. I love him so much."

"Actually, I have some choices that I have to make regarding where my life is going, too." Lori said. "My high school friend, well, truth be told he was much more than just a friend, showed up after six years. That's who you saw me with at the party. Right after graduation he went to Florida to study something about ocean life. He always was good at biology and stuff like that. Anyway, he graduated and landed a great job doing research at a private institution near Clearwater. He wants me to move there with him and maybe get married. He has some contacts at a TV station in Tampa, and they may have a job for me there. He's leaving in a few days and wants me to come down and stay with him. I have a week of vacation time, so I think I'm going to look around and check it out."

"Lori, that sounds great for you. Good luck."

"You too, Nick."

CHAPTER 22

About a week later a rather thick envelope arrived from Larry in Washington. In it was the standard broadcasting industry application for employment, a vacancy announcement for a Television Broadcast Technician and some information about G.N.N. The application was pretty intense and took a lot of time to fill out. The position was a journeyman level pay grade, about five thousand dollars more per year than he was currently getting paid. It was looking better all the time. Nick eagerly completed the paperwork and mailed it back to Larry almost immediately. He arranged to fly to Washington on his next long weekend, which was in about five weeks. All Susan knew at this time was that Nick was going to visit Larry and see D.C. for a little rest and recreation. Of course this plan met strong opposition. It meant that Susan had to be a full-time mom for five whole days! What was she going to do, get pissed off and leave? It was a no lose situation as Nick saw it.

The day had come, and Nick was at the arrival gate at Washington National Airport, standing there waiting was Larry.

"Welcome to the Nation's Capitol." Larry announced. "How was your flight?"

"Short," was all he could reply. Here he was in D.C. He hadn't been here since he was in high school.

"How would you like a little auto tour before we head to my place?"

"Sounds great. Let's go."

Larry explained all of the sights as they passed them one after another. When they passed the White House, Nick's heart skipped a beat. Right here in the middle of town was the White House! To the right was the Washington Monument. He could only imagine what it would be like to live here and see these things on a daily basis. And to have a job with banker's hours, Monday through Friday and have holidays off, to boot? It was almost too good to be true.

Just past the White House, the road joined Pennsylvania Avenue. There it was, directly before him, the Capitol Building. It was getting towards evening, so the partially setting sun gave the white marble a pinkish cast. After passing the FBI Building, Department of Justice, and many other places that he heard of on a daily basis on national news, Larry circled back on Independence Avenue, past the Lincoln Memorial and on to the George Washington Memorial Parkway. Larry's house was about a twenty-five minute ride from D.C, in Northern Virginia. Nick was pretty tired by the time they reached the house, so it wasn't too long after dinner and some obligatory family chit chat, that Nick excused himself and went up to the guest room. He had a busy day tomorrow and wanted to be sharp when he met the Chief Engineer.

The room was comfortable, but he had a problem in settling in. Lying in the dark, like a cinematic event, the thoughts of the day were replayed upon the screen of his mind's eye. These were cross faded into visions of Adam, Susan, and Lori. The visions were a mixture of things that once were and things to be. Was this all an act of desertion, a geographic cure? He couldn't help but to hear the words of his mother warning, "Remember, no matter where you go, there you are."

Nick didn't remember sleeping, but he must have. For, what seemed like only twenty minutes after closing his eyes, there was a knock on the guest room door.

"Rise and shine, pal. Time to get moving."

After a long groan, stretch and scratch, all Nick could muster was a weak, "I'm up."

"I got a hot cup of coffee here for ya, and the shower is all, yours. We have to leave in about forty five minutes."

"Thanks, Larry. I'll be right down."

Nick got out of bed and opened the door. Right there on the floor was a steaming mug of coffee, which he picked up and placed on the night stand. After a hot shower, shave and coffee, he was ready to go.

Larry and Nick met the carpool and headed into town. They were dropped off at the National Archives, two blocks from the building that housed the television service of G.N.N.

CHAPTER 23

After walking through the glass doors of the ten story building, they soon came to the guard's post where after showing his company ID, Larry signed Nick in. After clipping on his daily pass, Nick followed Larry to a secured area, which had a door that was opened by Larry's touching his ID to a sensor to the right of the door handle. Immediately after touching the sensor which had a small pulsating red light, there was a buzzing sound as Larry pulled the door open. Nick was quite impressed with this. He had only seen this in the movies, when secret agents entered the CIA, or some other highly secret and secure structure. To the right was a large opened area where the receptionist sat. There were several offices within this space.

"Happy Monday, Jan." Larry said to the receptionist.

"Happy Monday to you too, Larry," Jan replied.

"I brought a friend to meet Fred and take a look around. This is Nick. I used to work with him before I came here."

"Nice to meet ya, Nick. Let me see if Fred is back from the cafeteria yet."

Just then, Fred entered the office area carrying a bagel and coffee.

"Morning Fred." Larry greeted, "I have someone that I want you to meet. Fred, this is Nick. He's the one that I talked to you about."

"Nice to meet you. I've heard a lot about you. I'd shake your hand, but I'd spill this coffee all over both of us in the process. Come on in."

Fred walked to his desk and set down his breakfast. "Now for the handshake."

After shaking hands, Fred sat behind his desk while Larry and Nick took seats in front.

"So, tell me about yourself." Fred said as he took a bite of bagel and a gulp of coffee. After shaking his head, Fred said "You don't get coffee like this at home." Then after a short pause he said, "Thank god."

Nick feeling more relaxed, gave an oral resume, sparing the personal details. After about fifteen minutes of this, Fred said, "Sounds good. Larry, why don't you show Nick around, meet the guys and let's see if there is enough to lure you here."

Nick thanked Fred, then Larry took Nick on the tour.

Nick was amazed at what he saw. The studios and equipment equaled the major networks. So did the technicians. As a matter of fact, most of them had come from the networks in search of regular hours and less pressure. They, too, had become tired of the new "cheap and dirty" attitude in broadcasting, where the quality of the production was less important than the making of the money.

As they passed one of the control rooms, Nick noticed that the technical director was sitting back in his chair with his feet resting on the video switcher console, eating his breakfast. He was watching one of PBS's morning children's programs on the control room monitor.

"Now I know that this is where I want to work." Nick said, smiling at Larry.

"We work hard and relax hard here." Larry said, "It's like being a fireman. There isn't always something to do, but at a moment's notice we may be doing something at the White House or State Department. Don't worry, this will all change when we get our global satellite network going. That's why we are gearing up."

Nick was sure that this is what he wanted. Tuesday was a different day and a different attitude. Nick was filled with optimism and wanted to yell it to the world. He knew that it wasn't a sure thing yet, and he had to keep things under wraps for a while longer.

CHAPTER 24

It was now a month since his visit to Washington. Nick didn't have to leave for work until the late afternoon so he was there when the mail arrived. There, amid the bills and other junk mail was an official looking large envelope. It contained the security paperwork. Nick couldn't open it quickly enough and almost tore the papers inside in his haste to tear open the envelope. Since the position required a security clearance, the questions were extensive and required information that Nick had forgotten a long time ago, like addresses going back to his birth. With the help of his mother, he collected the required information. Nick was also required to take some blank fingerprint cards to his local police station and have them fill the blanks with his very own and personal black smudges. He couldn't wait to call Larry and tell him that the security packet was complete and on its way back to Washington. Larry told Nick that this was a good sign, that if they weren't really serious about hiring him, they wouldn't go to the expense of the extensive security check.

Four weeks later an investigator came to town to interview Nick in person at the Federal Building downtown. At each step Nick's optimism grew. Then, one afternoon while working in tele-cine, the master control booth phone rang.

"Nick, it's for you!" the master control technician shouted out the door.

Nick walked into the booth and took the phone. The tech left Nick alone and closed the door.

"This is Nick speaking."

"This is Valencia calling from G.N.N. Personnel. We would like to offer you a position as a Television Broadcast Technician with a starting salary of $35,000 a year. Are you still interested in the position?"

Nick wanted to yell, *Fuckin' A!,* but opted for an excited, "I sure am."

"Very good. You should be getting an official offer letter in the mail in a few days. Would you be able to start in three weeks?"

Now, in a flash, there were a million things going through his mind of things that first needed to be done. "Uh, yes. I guess I can."

"Excellent. The letter will contain details of where to report, when, etc. See you in a few weeks."

Nick didn't even remember saying thank you. He just hung up the phone and walked out of the master control booth in a daze. He excused himself and went for a coffee before he went to talk to Malloy. He couldn't believe that he was about to give notice of resignation, let alone what a change his life would be taking in just a few weeks. After a few moments alone, the impact of what just occurred seemed to start sinking in. He went back upstairs and entered Malloy's office.

"Malloy, you got a minute?"

"Sure Nick, what you got on your mind?"

"This is pretty hard for me to say. Ya know, I've been working here for about fifteen years. Well, I've been offered a job in D.C working with Larry, and I feel like I have to take it."

"Wow. I understand, Nick. I know you haven't been your good old happy self around here for a while. I wish there was something I could do to keep you here. When do you have to report there?"

"In a few weeks. I'm gonna really miss you guys. There's just a lot of shit happening in my life right now, and I feel like this is the best thing for me right now. Thanks for fifteen great years. You know I'll keep in touch."

"I know you will, Nick. Have a great life." They shook hands, and Nick left to go back to tele-cine. Now the hard part faced him. How to tell Susan and worst of all, how to tell Adam.

The next morning Nick got up when he heard Susan walking around upstairs after her shower. His heart pounded in his throat at the anticipation of what the next few minutes would be like. He dressed and went upstairs, where he smelled the fresh coffee. He usually waited until he heard Susan leave before he came upstairs, so this felt really strange. He was sitting at the table when Susan walked into the kitchen. Adam was still in his room, hopefully asleep. Nick didn't have to be at work until later this afternoon, so he would have time to talk to Adam later alone.

"What brings you out of the cave so early? Surely not to kiss your gorgeous wife good-bye and to bid her a good day. Or did you just get home from taking your teen love to school?"

Susan's acid tongue and sarcasm made what he had to tell her even easier. Her hair was still wet and hung straight down the back of her embroidered western shirt. She unbuttoned and unzipped her tight jeans so that she could tuck her shirt in. Nick couldn't imagine, considering how tight her jeans were that there was even room for a shirt tail in there. His sarcasm took over as he thought that there was always room when she wanted something to get into her pants, but he held his tongue this time. He could see the top edge of her bikini underwear as she tucked, zipped and buttoned.

"I have to tell you something important."

"Well make it fast. I have to get to work."

"You can wait a few goddamn minutes. Daddy isn't going to fire you for being late."

"All right." She whined in protest "What's so damn important?"

"I wanted to tell you that I am moving."

"Moving. What do you mean, moving? The bar in Hotel Basement isn't good enough for you any more? Moving where?"

"Away."

"Quit fucking with me. I don't have time for this."

"That's your problem, Susan. You never have time for what is really important. I'm moving to Washington. I have a job there."

"You have a what, where? And what the fuck am I and Adam supposed to do?"

"That's Adam and I. You always put yourself first, don't you. I have a job that starts in three weeks."

"Well, fuck me!" Susan yelled. "Ain't that just like you. Gets a little tough and you run away. Where am I supposed to live? I can't pay for this place, even with child support. Boy, are you going to pay, too."

"I guess we'll have to sell this place, and you'll just have to get an apartment. I'll just take whatever is mine and leave everything else with you."

"You bet your ass, you will. By the time I'm done with you you'll be lucky to have your ass!" Susan screamed.

"I have a good idea, let Adam come with me, and you and your shit-kicker can go out and make your own home on the range."

With that, Susan picked up her coffee mug and threw it at Nick. Nick ducked in time to hear it crash and shatter along with the microwave door. The next thing he heard was a loud "Fuck you!" as the door slammed and shortly thereafter the screeching of tires.

Nick turned his head to see the damage and saw Adam standing in the kitchen doorway holding a teddy bear in one hand and his favorite blanket in the other. How long had been standing there and how much did he hear? As loud as Susan was, the next county must have heard. Nick picked Adam up and held him close. His eyes welled up with tears as he carried him back to his room and sat with him on his little bed.

"Adam, Daddy has something to talk to you about."

"Are you going away, Daddy? Can I go with you?"

"Yes, sweetheart, Daddy is moving away, and I'm sorry, but you can't come with me right now."

"When will I see you?"

"Daddy will be getting a really nice place and I won't be that far away. You can come and visit, and we will be able to do all kinds of things together and have a lot of fun. There will be beaches to go to and zoos. Lots of stuff. And I will write to you all the time, ok?"

"Ok, Daddy. I love you."

"Daddy loves you too. How about we guys go out and get some pancakes, just me and you?"

"I like pancakes!" Nick helped Adam dress and out they went. Nick knew that starting this very moment, every second that he could spend with Adam from now on would be the best ever.

CURRENT EVENTS
THE 1990S
PART 2

CHAPTER 1

The weather in Lauderdale was exceptionally warm for early spring, and the sun was only minutes away from peeking over the horizon. Lori, having been very restless during the night, quietly rolled out of bed, picked up the novel that she had started reading the evening before, and went to the kitchen where she poured a glass of fresh grapefruit juice. The third floor condominium that she shared with her husband, John, was across the street from the beach so it afforded a beautiful view and the relaxing surf sounds of the Atlantic Ocean. There was a glass enclosed sun deck that was accessed through a sliding door in the living room, and it was here that she headed. Lori set the book and glass of juice down onto the white wicker end table and went to open the window. The warm breeze entered, carrying with it the fresh smell of the ocean and the feeling of serenity. Before going back to the matching wicker sofa, she took a moment to close her eyes and inhale deeply, then slowly exhaling as she opened her eyes. In just the time that it took her to re-open her eyes, a slight amber glow appeared on the horizon where the water met the sky. She sat Indian style on the sofa. Her nightwear consisted only of an extra large t-shirt with a picture of a dolphin on the front. Since they lived on the third floor and facing the ocean, there was little concern of anyone peeping. She loved the way the warm breeze caressed her arms and legs, and gently lifted her long, silky hair to whisper good morning into her tingling ears.

The sun, reaching higher into the sky now, silhouetted a formation of pelicans heading north. Lori really loved it here for the most part. It was certainly beautiful, and she loved her dolphins. It was the feeling of loneliness that bothered her the most. She felt that she left everything behind to move to the east with John. Television jobs were scarce, and if there was one, it wasn't a technical position like she once had. The "girl" jobs in TV were usually secretarial, or receptionists, and there was no way she wanted to say "Do you want fries with that?" The holiday trips back home didn't seem like enough time to ease the loneliness. Lori felt trapped here in Florida.

The move to Lauderdale at first was very exciting for both Lori and John. For Lori, it was living in a place to where everyone else came for fun, for the variety of delicious foods, music, and the beach. For John, it was all of that plus the job of his dreams. He worked, played with and studied sea turtles, dolphins, birds, and a seemingly endless variety of ocean life. At this point in his job he was sometimes required to be away for periods of time, sometimes for weeks, aboard research vessels or at study locations. They spent vacation times together, but it never seemed like John was ever able to entirely leave the job behind and to devote the quality time just to her that she felt that she desperately needed.

So, for now, she worked in a small non-chain book store on the beach boardwalk where she found an endless supply of books to carry her off and to escape into her own private places and adventures. She particularly liked the romance novels since it filled the space that was mostly vacant in her real life. Lori didn't have many friends that she could consider close friends. Through working at the bookstore she had made a lot of acquaintances, but as for someone who she could confide to, she turned to her boss and best friend, Pam.

The sun was higher in the sky now, and off in the distance Lori could hear the sounds of rush hour starting. John was awake now and in the kitchen making coffee. She could hear the sound of the coffee bean grinder. She set down her book and slid open the door to the living room. She could see John standing at the sink and could hear the music coming from the TV signaling the local news cut-in during the network morning news. She walked up behind him and put her arms around his waist. Startled, he turned his head around.

"Jesus, you just scared the shit out of me!"

"And a good morning to you, too."

"I woke up and you weren't there. Is everything okay?"

"I just couldn't sleep. I guess I have a lot on my mind. When do you have to leave?"

"I have about an hour, why?"

The combination of the book that she was reading and the calmness of the morning had put her into a rather romantic mood. What she wanted was for the two of them to go back into the bedroom for a good morning love making session. The length of time between love makings was getting longer and longer, and she felt that it was long past due.

"I was just wondering if you'd like to go back to bed for a, you know."

It used to be that merely the sight of her standing there with nothing on but a t-shirt was all that was needed to get things started.

"Lori, I just took a shower already, and I have a few things that I have to do before I go to the lab. Maybe this weekend."

"Sure. See you later."

John continued cutting his grapefruit and Lori headed back into the bedroom feeling frustrated and rejected...again. She laid there quietly while John finished dressing. As she watched him remove his robe, the memories of how things used to be between them appeared in her mind's eye like movie short subjects. Having finished dressing, John picked up his brief case, came over to her side of the bed and kissed her on the forehead.

"See ya later." he said, "Have a good day."

"You too."

He picked up his keys and exited the condo. All that remained was the lingering smell of the mix of his cologne and coffee.

CHAPTER 2

Lori had about an hour before she had to be at the bookstore. It was a quick fifteen minutes away, so she had time for a leisurely bath. She put one of her favorite CDs, lit a scented candle and took it into the bathroom where she placed it on the edge of the tub. While the water was filling the tub, she went back out to the sun deck to get her book. She often relaxed in the tub while reading, especially during those times when she found herself alone while John was away chasing his mermaids.

Lori pulled the t-shirt over her head, folded it, and put in on the bed. Turning toward the bathroom door, she looked at herself in the full length mirror. She stood there with her hands at her sides looking at the reflection of her nude body. She remembered the myth that television makes you look twenty pounds heavier. This wasn't TV and the extra pounds that she was looking at were real. In fact it was more like ten to fifteen pounds more than when they married. She was sure that this was the reason that she looked unattractive to John.

Lori picked up the book and carried it into the bathroom. The sandle wood scent of the candle began to relax her. She turned off the water and tested it with her toes. Determining that no adjustments to temperature were required, she stepped in and lowered herself into the large soaking tub. The water gave her a warm and welcoming hug as it surrounded her. She slid down until her hair floated and her head and knees were the only parts of her body above the water. She felt as if she could stay here all day. The only sounds were the CD playing what was referred to as "new age" and the occasional sound of a drop of water falling from the faucet at the opposite end of the tub and breaking the placidity with rings of concentric circles. She resumed reading her book at the point from where she left off, and before long she was back in the fantasyland of her mind. After reading only a couple chapters, she dropped the book on the floor next to the tub and reached for the bar of soap beside her. Lori lathered up her hands and gently washed her face. She slid farther down into the water so that her face was submerged, rinsing off the soap. When she raised back up, she had to remove her wet hair from her face. Her fingers ran through her hair. How she wished that it was someone other than herself doing this. After soaping her hands again, she gently ran them over her breasts. Immediately her nipples hardened, and she felt the electricity flow from there to a place deep between her legs. While her left hand continued to caress her breast, her right hand followed down her belly, lightly brushing across her pubic area and finding its spot between her now opened legs. Her hand worked in a circular motion until she spasmed with a pleasure that resulted in a complete release of tension and the greatest feelings of well being. The cooling water gently segued her back to the real world and the fact that she had to get dressed and go to work.

CHAPTER 3

When Lori arrived at the bookstore, Pam had just arrived and was unlocking the padlock that secured the security gate that covered the entire front of the store.

"Beautiful morning, aint it?" Pam asked with her twangy southern voice.

"Sure is." Lori answered, knowing secretly why on this morning she felt particularly good.

"How about you help me hoist this thing and I buy you a cup of coffee?"

Lori would have helped her even without the coffee bribe, but answered, "You got a deal if you toss in a cookie."

"Deal." Pam agreed as they both lifted the gate and locking it into the up position with the same lock.

"Tell you what, you go and get two coffees and a couple cookies and I'll open the store. Here's a five, that ought to cover it."

Lori took the five and almost skipped the two doors down where there was an opened air café serving breakfast on the beach. Upon her return, Pam not only had the store opened, but there were already some tourist customers milling about. Outside, on the boardwalk, joggers and bike riders were getting an early start so as to avoid the hottest time of the day. The French roast coffee was the perfect companion for the large oatmeal raisin cookies. At least oatmeal cookies made it seem like one was consuming something healthful.

"So, what do you guys have planned for the weekend? I know it's only Thursday, but you can't plan for the weekend too soon, now can you?" Pam asked.

"Well, I think John has something very romantic and exciting planned. NOT! Probably not much, really, just cleaning the place up and running some errands. The usual. What do you have going?"

Pam was single, pretty attractive, and rarely had a weekend where she wasn't going on a date or lacking something to do. "I have a hot one Saturday night. I think he's planning on an evening of dining and dancing Cuban style in Miami. Should be a hoot!"

Lori had confided several times to Pam about her love life, or lack thereof, and her feelings of being alone and trapped, so Pam tried to include her in some girl type activities. At those rare times when Pam didn't have the "hot one" she would ask Lori to see a movie with her, or go shopping and to lunch. Even when John was home during the weekend, there was little conversation or activities together. Yet, Lori spent the weekend at home since she had the old fashioned idea that if he was home, she should be there too.

"Hey, I have an idea. I'm invited to one of those marital aids and sex toy parties tonight at a friend's house. Why don't you come along?"

"Right. I have a great picture of that scene. I tell John, 'Honey, I know that we don't make love any more, but I really would like to go to this party tonight where they sell sex toys and marital aids.'"

"Who knows, there may be something there to help you in that area. Couldn't hurt, could it? Just think of it as a fun night out with the girls."

"Thanks for the invite. I'm sure it will be great fun and all, but I would be too embarrassed, anyway."

"No one will give a shit. You probably will never see most of them again anyway, at least think about it. I could pick you up about eight o'clock. Who knows, if it works, I'll even let you come to work a little late tomorrow. Now how's that for a deal?"

"Okay, I'll think about it but don't count on it. I've never even seen an X rated movie before let alone sex toys, for cripes sake."

It was about three o'clock, and things were pretty slow. Pam was checking out some customers at the register and Lori was putting some new books on the new release shelf when Lori's cell phone rang. The number that appeared on the caller ID was their home phone number.

"Hello?"

"Lori, it's John. Listen, I am calling from home. I came home to pack a few things. I have a short trip that I have to take for a few days, and I should be home either Sunday night or Monday depending on how things go. Sorry for the last minute notice."

"Are you going to be home for dinner, at least?"

"Sorry, hon, but we have to be on the boat by five. I'll have my cell on if you need to reach me."

"Sure, have a safe trip. See you in a few. Bye." Lori hit the off button on her phone and looked up to see Pam looking at her.

Lori must have had a very disappointed look on her face, because Pam asked "Everything ok? You look pretty down."

"Just the usual, John's off again, and I have another weekend alone to look forward to."

"We'll put a smile back on that face. Now there's no excuse for not coming to the party. C'mon, they're just a bunch of crazy babes having a good time and letting loose for a while."

"You win, I'll see you at eight."

"That's a girl!"

The rest of the time before closing seemed to drag. Lori wondered if she was doing the right thing, then she thought of herself sitting alone in the condo for the next four days.

CHAPTER 4

Lori was pretty nervous about the upcoming evening having no idea what to expect. Pam was right on time to pick her up and before you could say Steely Dan they were at her friend Tish's house. They reached the door and Tish, having seen them from the window, opened the door before Pam had a chance to ring the doorbell.
"Welcome y'all," Tish greeted.
"Tish, this is Lori. She could use some spirit lifting, so I brought her along. I figured that if this couldn't do it then nothing could."
"You're right on with that." Tish replied, "C'mon in and we'll start lifting those spirits with some spirits. What'll you have? I got it all."
"Do you have some white wine?" Lori asked.
"Comin' up. While I get your bev, why don't you go in and make yourself at home and introduce yourselves around."
Pam and Lori went into the living room where six other women were already drinking and snacking.
"Welcome to the party. I'm Brenda, your romance specialist for the evening." She handed both Pam and Lori her business cards. "I have some really great and exciting things to show you tonight, and we're going to have lots of fun."
Lori wasn't too sure of that, but she smiled as greetings and introductions were exchanged around the room. By this time Tish came in with a huge glass of wine.
"This should get you loosened up, honey. Enjoy!"
Lori took the glass of chilled wine and took a sip. It was just right, not too dry. Since Lori was so nervous about the evening, she didn't eat anything before Pam picked her up. As a result she began to feel the effects of the wine in very short order. She felt her cheeks redden and a slightly numbing sensation in her brain. Lori rarely drank alcohol, so this was quite a pleasant sensation.

Brenda, the romance specialist, began her presentation by placing a number of catalogues on the coffee table followed by a number of gadgets, both manually and electrically operated, lotions and other miscellaneous items. She announced that if there was anything desired that was not represented at the party, it would be available on line through their web site.

Lori couldn't believe some of the things she was seeing. One of the women picked up a huge rubber penis and displayed it to the group in a rather comical manner, as if she were showing can of furniture wax in a TV commercial. Everyone laughed as she proceeded to pass it around the room. "This also comes, no pun intended, in a vibrating model and if you prefer, in black," Brenda explained. The passing around of items to feel and smell continued for about an hour, ending with a video of many of the represented items being demonstrated. This video, Brenda noted, was also available for purchase. After much wine was consumed, a sensory overload of sex toys and marital aids, and lots of laughs, it was time to go home. Lori had a great time feeling that she had done something naughty tonight. She picked up the business card and her catalogue, said good night to her new friends, and she and Pam started home.

"So, what ya think?" Pam asked.

"It felt really great to just let it loose for a while and do something just for the fun of it."

"You act like you have never done anything crazy and spontaneous before. Have you?"

"Actually, in my younger days I did, once."

"Ooh. Tell Pammy about it."

"It was about twenty years ago when I worked at the television station. There was one of the techs that I was really attracted to, and I think he was pretty hot for me. I invited him over to my place late one night, and things got pretty steamy."

"Okay, don't stop now and don't spare any of the details."

"There really aren't any details. We got really close on the couch, and we kissed and touched and before it got to the point of no return, I cooled it."

"What happened to make you stop?"

"I don't know. Thinking back on it, if I knew then what I know now, maybe things would have been different. He kept wanting to know why and if we could get together again, and it made me feel pressured, so I backed off even more. Afterwards I tried to act like it never happened which made him feel more frustrated and probably pissed off at me. Then John came back into my life, and it helped me push it to the back of my mind, but I never forgot and always wondered."

"Wondered what?"

"You know, I wonder where he is and what he's doing, if he's married and if he even remembers me."

"You said wonder, not wondered. Do you still think about him?"

"I guess I do, especially during those times when I'm alone. I've even thought sometimes, of trying to find him."

"Then why don't you? You seem to enjoy being crazy and spontaneous now. I say, go for it. It's just two pals checking in after a long time. You know me, I'd have to know. Let me know what you find out. I can't wait!"

"Maybe I will, just for the hell of it."

Pam pulled up to the front door of the building. Lori thanked her again for a great time and headed up to her condo. Thoughts of Nick coming to the forefront again after all this time seemed exciting and scary at the same time. She decided to make some calls tomorrow, just for the heck of it.

CHAPTER 5

Lori kept putting off making the call until the next morning when Pam put the phone into her hand and said, "Now dial the damn number and get it over with. It ain't like you're calling the White House, for Christ sake."

"You're right," Lori responded, "that would be much easier."

Nervously, Lori punched in the phone number and after only a few rings the station's receptionist answered. Lori couldn't believe it when she heard a very familiar voice. "This is Vivian, how may I direct your call?" Vivian, the receptionist, worked there when Lori first started working at the station. She and Vivian had quite a special relationship since, as Vivian often reminded her, 'We girls have to stick together around here.' It was Vivian who kept her apprised of the station gossip and about who was screwing who and other valuable and necessary girl stuff.

"Hello Vivian, this is Lori. I used to work there. Do you remember me?"

"Well, I'll be goddamned. Lori honey, of course I remember you! Where in the hell are you and how you doin'?"

"I'm doing fine. I'm married now and live in Lauderdale. How about you? I can't believe you're still working there."

"I'm still kicking. Honey, I know where too many of the bones are hanging around here for them to get rid of old Vivie. What brings a call from you after all this time?"

"Well, I feel pretty funny asking you this, but are there any of the old guys that worked there when I did still around? I'm curious about where Nick might be, and I thought that maybe he has been in contact with some of the old guys over the years."

"Nick, huh, I seem to recall that that boy had a sort of thing for you. Funny you should bring that up. Nick was here about six months ago, and he and Alan went to lunch together. Let me ring you up to

Master Control and see if Alan is there. Honey, don't be a stranger. When you're up here, I'd love to see ya."

"Thanks a lot, Vivian. Will do, I promise."

With that Lori heard a click followed by the ringing to another location.

"Master Control, this is Chuck"

"May I please speak to Alan?"

"Hold on a second and I'll see if he's still here."

Lori heard the distant sound of one of the afternoon soaps over the phone as it lay on the console. "This is Alan."

"Hello Alan, this is a voice from your past. It's Lori. Remember me?"

"Remember you? How can anyone ever forget a chick as beautiful as you! What's up?"

"That's one of the sweetest lies that I've heard in a long time. Thanks."

"My pleasure...I wish. Oh well, like I ever had a chance. What brings such a pretty voice to my ear?"

"Well, I have a question for you."

"Is it a personal question? The answer is yes. Whatever you heard is true."

"Actually, I was wondering if you know where I could reach Nick."

"Now you really broke my heart. I thought you wanted me after all these years. I've gotten better with age, you know."

"Yeah, I know. So has your bullshit. So? Have you heard from Nick?"

"Well as a matter of fact he was here not too long ago and gave me one of his business cards. Hold on a second and let me get it out of my wallet. Okay, here it is. I have his work e-mail and phone number. Which one do you want?"

"I'll take both."

Alan read the info to her and added, "Funny thing, but when he was here, he asked if anyone heard from you?"

"Thanks a lot, Alan. Tell anyone that's still there that might remember me that I said hello."

"Will do. Good to hear your voice. Take care."

"You too. Bye."

Pam was almost as excited as Lori was as she watched Lori write down the numbers. "Ain't that some shit?" Pam said excitedly. You gonna call him? Call him now. C'mon!"

"Don't get your panties in a knot. Maybe I'll send him an e-mail and see what happens."

"Maybe my ass. You'll do it tonight."

"Maybe," Lori said more emphatically.

Lori thought about it for the rest of the day and into the evening. About eleven o'clock that night she couldn't stand the internal dialoging, those two voices inside of her head playing point, counterpoint any more. The more she tried to fall asleep the more it kept her awake. Not being able to sleep, she got out of bed and logged on to the internet and into her e-mail. She clicked on "compose" and typed the very short message. She sat there staring at it for what seemed like forever until she decided to click on "send." She slowly pushed the left side of the mouse as if it would give her time to change her mind before it raced at the speed of light along the internet superhighway. Before she realized that the slow pressure on the mouse had finally made contact, she was startled by the "Message Sent Successfully" alert. "Well, it's too late to turn back now." she said, with a mixed sense of relief and the wondering if somehow she had just done a very wrong thing.

CHAPTER 6

It was the start of what would become a beautiful spring day in the Nation's Capitol. The light of the early rising sun stirred Nick as it shone through the break in the bedroom drapes. The alarm was set to go off at six thirty, just five minuets from now. One of the benefits of being a manager was that you didn't have to be at work at O dark hundred. You had supervisors working for you that did that. Nick reached over to his nightstand and switched off the alarm so that it wouldn't awaken his wife, Meg. Meg stirred when she sensed that he was awake and rolled over to her left side so that she was facing Nick as he rolled back after the disarming was complete.

"Good morning sweetheart." she said softly and closely enough to his ear so that he could feel her breathe. She gave Nick a gentle kiss on the lips.

"Good morning to you, sweetie," he said as he returned the kiss. Nick still had a few minutes before he had to hit the shower. The car pool wasn't due for an hour, so he laid there quietly on his back with his hands behind his head. "So, what do you have planned for the day?" he asked Meg. Meg worked from home as a free-lance writer for one of the major newspapers in the area, so her hours were mostly driven by the needs of the individual project that she was working on.

"Well, I have to be in Reston for a lunch interview with a developer who is planning the major addition of high-tech companies to the area, sort of making it the Silicon Valley of the east. After that I may just hang around there and get some local reactions. I should be home by four thirty or so."

Nick was very proud of Meg. She wasn't only very creative and intelligent but quite attractive as well. Most importantly, she loved Adam and the three cats that he brought into their union. She was very different than what he had been used to. Their three cats, who shared the bed and slept either on or between Nick and Meg, were now awake and ready for their breakfast. The eldest of the three, a Maine Coon named Disa, had just taken up position on Nick's chest and began the purr and paw massage ritual clearly designed to motivate him to his feet. Although not formally educated, she did possess an M.F.A., Master of the Feline Arts, having mastered purring, paw massaging, and head butting.

"Well, I guess you have your orders," Meg mused, "You better get moving. No telling what you may find in your shoe later if you don't."

Nick exuded a grunt as he lifted himself out of the bed and donned his robe. Disa then leaped from the bed and led him along the route to the fridge, ears aimed to the rear making sure that Nick didn't stray from the path. The other two, younger by thirteen years, a tortie named Pikabo, pronounced peek-a-boo, and a very assertive calico, named Simca, followed suit by jumping from their spots on the bed and joining the parade. It was a short but difficult trip due to the weaving of three felines between and around his legs.

Having taken care of their "children," Nick proceeded to complete his morning routine, starting with the teeth, then face, then shower. He usually ran on automatic at this point, and any interruption to the routine made him feel somewhat disoriented. Meg, knowing this stayed in bed watching the early news and weather, keeping out of his way. Breakfast was also pretty routine: a small bowl of cold cereal and milk. This was just something to get his day started, since after arrival at work there was a pre-work coffee meeting with some of his colleagues.

It was nearly seven thirty and the calico, Simca, had just finished her job of lapping up the last of his cereal bowl milk, leaving the smallest of cereal remains lining the bottom of the bowl. Now, and only now, was Nick was allowed to pick up the bowl, rinse it and put it into the dishwasher. As he was placing his arm into the sleeve of his coat, he heard the familiar beep of the carpool horn.

"I'm outa here, sweetie!" Nick called back to Meg.

"Have a good day!" Meg answered. Nick took one last look around to make sure that all three cats were accounted for. All three, having finished their breakfast, were now curled up in their favorite spots resting up for a full day of squirrel and bird watching action. He carefully exited and secured the door behind himself.

Robert, who was sitting in the passenger side, opened the door of the car and released the seat latch enabling Nick to squeeze into the back seat.

After the round of morning salutations, Nick settled back and closed his eyes for the forty-minute ride into town. As he drifted off into a semi-conscious state, the last thing that he remembered was the voice of the morning shock jock on the radio. The rule was that it was the driver's choice of where the radio was tuned for the commute.

It seemed like only five minutes had passed when Nick awoke to the sounds of downtown rush hour in the big city, honking horns, blaring sirens, and screeching tires. Thus began another day, a day like any other day. The carpool came to rest in its assigned space in the underground garage. The doors opened simultaneously and the occupants emerged, a little stiff, a little wrinkled but for the most part, none the worse for wear. After bidding each other a good day, all four went their separate ways. Nick was the only one to stay in the building, exiting the garage through a secured door, which required a password to open. Once on the other side of the door, he had one more leg of the journey to go, the elevator up to the fourth floor and to his office. Nick's continued running on automatic mode, checking the phone for any messages while the computer booted up after logging in. There were no message beeps coming from the telephone handset. That was a good thing, since it meant that no one was calling in sick for the day, at least yet. By now the computer had fully awakened and was ready for the password command for e-mail. As Nick entered the last two digits of the super secret password, Jeff, one of Nick's colleagues, leaned into the office doorway and knocked on the metal doorframe.

"You ready?" Jeff asked.

"Hell yeah!" was the reply as Nick arose from behind his desk, reaching for his jacket, which was hanging on the back of his chair. He finished putting on the jacket as he and Jeff headed out the door and toward the elevator. The office door closed behind them as the computer signaled with a special tone that alerted "new messages." This in itself was certainly not an uncommon occurrence. Nick often had at least twenty new messages each morning, a lot of jokes from other colleagues and perhaps even some important, business related mail. What was very different about today's e-mail bag was from where one of these messages had been sent and from whom.

CHAPTER 7

The usual meeting place was a diner across the street, where one could get a decent cup of coffee and killer fried potatoes with onions, a combination guaranteed to get you going, sometimes in more than one way. The morning coffee counted as a business meeting, since it was attended by managers of at least three different branches of the TV technical service. Although most of the conversation was the usual bullshit, it was surprising how much necessary information was shared. Nick was always amused by the fact that although he worked for a communications medium, how much of a lack of communications there really was. Working for such a large corporation meant that there were reams of paperwork generated, except for what you really needed to know to get the job done. It seemed that no one in upper management could make a decision to save his ass, let alone commit something to paper.

Nick opened the glass door and let Jeff enter first. There was nothing like the smell of fresh coffee and bacon to start both the day and one's appetite. It didn't matter what Nick had to eat earlier, there was always room for a couple strips of bacon and fried potatoes. It was relatively quiet except for the low level mix of many conversations, the occasional clinking of glass and the sizzle of the grill.

Sitting near the back in a booth were Mike, from video tape, and Bill, from master control.

"Mornin' gents." Bill greeted. "C'mon over and share some vittles and intelligent conversation."

"Yeah, right. If it was intelligent conversation that I was after, I would be sitting in the corner talking to myself," Nick joked. Nick slid over to the window side of the booth bench, and Jeff slid in next to him.

A menu was unnecessary since the specials, which by the way, were the same every day, were written on a dusty chalkboard hanging on the wall over the fry grill.

Maryann, the waitress and owner's niece, headed toward their booth, order pad in hand. Maryann was in her mid to late twenties, had shoulder length blonde hair which she had fixed into a French braid, and a great figure that she brought attention to by wearing a diner logo t-shirt that was at least two sizes too small. Clearly it was more than the food that attracted the guys to the diner

"Happy Friday boys." She greeted. "What'll you have?"

Mike barely got the first syllable out when Bill cut him off. "Careful Mike, she means for breakfast."

"Thank you for clearing that up for me, shit for brains. Now, may I continue? "Mike turned back to Maryann, who had a big smile on her face. She had a great sense of humor and could give it back as well as take it. "What do you recommend, sweetheart?" he queried.

"Well, let me see. The eggs Benedict are superb today, as are the lobster omelets. I might also suggest the French toast with fresh strawberries."

"It all sounds so delightful, so many choices."

"How's this for a choice Mr.Trump, shit on a shingle, take it or leave it."

"I'll take it."

Maryann turned next to Nick who ordered his usual two strips of bacon and the killer home fries. Jeff ordered a fried egg sandwich with a side of home fries, and Bill ordered a western omelet.

Maryann automatically brought each one of them a cup of coffee and went back behind the counter to wait for their orders to come up.

"I hate to talk business, but have any of you heard anything about a feed from the White House south lawn on Monday?" Nick asked.

Mike took a gulp of coffee. "I heard something about that, but I haven't seen any paperwork on it yet?"

"They haven't told me shit, and I'm the one who will have to schedule a field production crew. I'm always the last to know," Nick said.

"All I know is that the President of France is visiting, and there may be an outdoor arrival ceremony, weather permitting," Bill said. "I don't know yet if it's a pool feed or if we're going to provide the switched feed. Mike, do you know anything?"

Mike broke into an impish smile. "Yeah, I got bad news and good news."

"Okay, smart ass," Jeff said impatiently," give us the bad news first."

"The bad news is that I have no idea what you are talking about."

"And the good news?" Jeff asked more impatiently.

"Good news is that I am getting laid this weekend!"

"Well, thanks so much for sharing. Please allow me to speak for the group, Mike, when I tell you how happy we all are for you," Jeff replied.

Mike was the only one of the group who was not married and seemingly had a one tracked mind. Almost all of his conversations turned to sex more sooner than later. "I'm so happy that you all are so happy. After all, it's been about a month."

"You mean with a woman, or by yourself?" Nick asked.

"Very funny, my friend. I don't play with myself any more because I'm afraid I'll give myself something."

"Poor baby, I feel so bad for you," Bill remarked, "A month? I've been married for fifteen years. Hell, that would be something that I would be bragging about!"

With that, they all started laughing, Nick nearly expelling his coffee through his nose.

Maryann arrived with a tray full of breakfast plates. "Sounds like you boys are having way too much fun over here."

"Don't worry," said Nick "This is the best that it gets. As soon as we leave here, it will all be down hill from there."

"Sorry to hear that. Y'all have a great weekend, and I'll see you all on Monday."

"You too," They all said. Now they all set into the serious business of breakfast.

After Nick drank his last gulp of coffee he said, "Well, I better get back and see if I can find out anything about Monday. Maybe the e-mailman delivered something useful overnight."

With that they all picked up their checks, left tip money and headed out for their respective offices. Fridays were known as "anything can happen day," since upper management often procrastinated, leaving much unfinished business until the end of the week and now it was deadline time. Shit rolls downhill, and Nick and his colleagues were just about at the bottom.

Nick found the key to his office on the key ring and unlocked the office door. He used the coat tree that sat just inside the door as a doorstop, propping it open. He walked to the business side of his desk and hung his coat over the back of his chair. Now, first things first, he turned his radio on to the classic rock station. After a minor tuning adjustment, he was ready to meet the day head on. Still no messages on the phone, so that meant that the next scheduled shift was probably going to be intact. Next, with a slight movement of the computer mouse the screen saver disappeared and the e-mail list popped up. As expected, there were the several junk e-mails from the same people as always. They were immediately deleted since there really wasn't time to trudge through pages of old jokes that he had probably already had heard or read. Still nothing from the Traffic Department regarding the White House field production. One particular e-mail was not from the usual joke sender or any other addressee that he recognized, and he could see from the address that it clearly wasn't from an internal address.

CHAPTER 8

"Dolphinlover" was the e-mail address that caught Nick's eye. The subject line read "Is this you?" With some degree of apprehension, he moved the cursor over the message and clicked on it. All that the message read was "Are you the one who worked at the TV station back in Ohio?" Now his curiosity really had peaked. He knew whom he would have liked to hear from, but that seemed pretty unlikely, since it was about twenty years since Lori, and during that time he often checked to see if he could find her with no results. He knew that she had moved to Florida a long time ago but not exactly where. The visions of her beautiful face and memory of that night had replayed in his mind often, especially when he saw someone who resembled her on the subway or walking along the streets of D.C. "Well, nothing ventured, nothing gained." Nick said softly to himself as he clicked on "reply." His reply was short and direct: "Yes, I did work at a TV station in Ohio. Why and who would like to know?" Nick hit "send" and knew that until he got a response he would be more than just a little anxious.

~

This same morning also found Lori in quite an anxious state sitting on the love seat in her living room reading her book and sipping a hot cup of herbal tea. She had a real problem in concentrating this morning and still didn't know what the paragraph said after reading it three times. She had another restless night last night partially due to the fact that she was home alone again, and mostly because she couldn't believe what she had done the night before. Lori picked up the cordless phone that was sitting on the end table and called Pam at the bookstore.
"Boardwalk Books," Pam greeted.

"Hi Pam, this is Lori."

"Hi sweetie, what's going on? You okay?"

"Yeah, I guess I'm all right. I had a really rough night last night and didn't sleep too well. I'm having a really hard time getting it together this morning. Would you have a problem if I came in a couple hours late this morning?"

"I guess not, it's not too busy this morning. The really important question is did you send the e-mail?"

"Well, as a matter of fact I did. I'll tell you all about it when I get in."

"Now I can't wait! See you soon."

"Thanks, Pam. You're the best!"

"Yeah, I know. Go get an hour's sleep. Bye."

Lori got up from the love seat and started pacing. She had no idea of where she was headed, just that she had this extra energy that made her feel the need to keep moving for no apparent reason or destination. As she reached the desk where the computer sat, she stopped as if some impenetrable force field kept her from moving any farther. She just stood there and stared at it for what seemed like a long time. As if on it's own, her finger reached out and depressed the start button which brought the computer to life. As several different sounds emanated from the box and the screen lit up, she pulled the desk chair out and sat down. Soon the noises ceased and the screen settled in to reveal several icons, one of which was only one click away from the e-mail. The computer dialed the phone and soon she heard the distinctive sound of two computers shaking hands and exchanging greetings and information. "You have 3 new messages," the video alert read. Her heart began to race as she opened the mailbox and saw that one of them was a reply from Nick. This time there was no procrastinating a reply. The words, "It's Lori just checking in. Would love to hear from you if you have the time," flew from the keyboard and into cyberspace in record time.

Contact had been made and their lives, although very different now, have touched again.

CHAPTER 9

"If I have the time? Jesus, I've been waiting and wondering for almost twenty years. Of course I have time," Nick said aloud and quite excitedly upon receipt of Lori's reply. He couldn't wait to talk to her, even if only by computer. He immediately fired off another cyber salvo to her. It read, "I can't believe it's you. Whatever made you want to contact me after all this time? I have so much that I want to talk to you about. I could go on for hours. Looking forward to hearing from you SOON!" Although he knew it was unrealistic to expect a reply only minutes after he sent his message he still checked for new messages whenever he had a minute to spare throughout the day.

~

Lori hadn't yet received this latest message from Nick, since she was already on her way to the bookstore when it was sent, but she couldn't wait to see Pam and tell her what had transpired. When she arrived, Pam was just finishing up with a customer. After closing the cash drawer Pam asked, "Okay, tell me what happened, and remember no details spared."

"Well, I sent the e-mail and got an answer this morning."

"That's it? What did you say and what did he say. Jesus, what do I have to do to pull information out of you?"

"A cup of coffee and a valium would help."

"Will a warm soda and a Midol work?"

"I just asked if it was him that worked at the TV station."

"Like you didn't know. Go on."

"Then he said that he was and who wanted to know."

"You didn't even tell him who you were? At least I'm not the only one who has to pull shit out of you. Is that it?"

"Then I wrote him back and said it was me and to write back if he had time. I didn't get a response from that one yet."

"Don't you feel great? I'd be floating on a cloud by now."

"No doubt, I feel charged, but I feel sort of guilty at the same time."

"Guilty? About what? Sending an e-mail to an old friend?"

"I'd feel different if there wasn't, you know, a thing about it."

"A thing? Sweetie, you need to get out more. If I remember correctly, the truth is that you *almost*, as you say, had a thing. And so what even if you did have a *thing*? That was a long time ago and in a world far away."

"I know, but I guess I feel like I'm being sneaky behind John's back or something."

"Look. If it makes you feel good, do it. You spend enough time feeling bad about being lonely and ignored. If this adds a little spice here and there, what's the problem. It's not like you're doing *it* or anything."

"Actually, I haven't done *it* with anyone but John, if you must know."

"Baby, this could really get interesting! Just remember, Pam needs details."

"Jesus, Pam, are you trying to scare the shit out of me, or what?"

This line of questioning was interrupted by the sound of the door opening and another customer coming in. Lori couldn't wait to get home and check her e-mail. At least now she had more to look forward to that just sitting around waiting for John…again.

~

The workday seemed like twenty-four hours long until the time came for Nick to meet the carpool to go home. It pained him to have to log off the computer for the weekend without having heard one last time from Lori. He knew that he would go crazy for the next two days not knowing if there was another e-mail waiting. Nick's old insecurities started taking over as he wondered to himself if perhaps the reason that she hadn't written him back yet was that he probably had scared her off. He remembered that she didn't like to be pressured, and maybe he was asking too much. He hoped for one more chance to slow things down and to gain her trust. It was like trying to get close to a frightened bunny. But for now it was important to just relax and see what Monday would bring. The tough part would be to share the weekend with Meg and have Lori on his mind at the same time. He loved Meg to death and shared what some would consider the perfect life and now the memories of a past infatuation were creeping into their very private space. Nick wondered if there would be room for both at the same time. His mind began the all too familiar thermal runaway again. *What the hell am I thinking, for god's sake,* he thought, *It's just an e-mail and I'm making a whole love affair out of it.* He shook his head and smiled as he closed his office door for the weekend and headed for the carpool.

~

Lori just finished checking out the last customer and Pam took the cash drawer to the back. Before long the lights were switched off, the door locked, and the gate pulled down and locked. Lori and Pam exchanged best wishes for a good weekend, and they each went their own way. Pam headed for the bank with the day's deposit, and Lori for her condo and a weekend to do some pondering and perhaps travel to some romantic getaway through the pages of her book.

CHAPTER 10

On Fridays a flower vendor set up shop in the lobby of Nick's building, and Nick picked up a bunch of red roses to take home to Meg. She always loved it when he walked in with flowers. It started raining that afternoon, so the normally slow D.C. Friday traffic was even worse than usual. Nick was settled into his spot in the back seat and was so pre-occupied in thought that he didn't hear any of the carpool conversation or the radio. The carpool finally pulled up in front of Nick's house at about six thirty. After a round of wishes for a good weekend, Nick exited the car and held the flowers horizontally over his head to block as much rain as possible and ran to the front door. The roof overhang afforded him shelter from the rain as he placed the bunch of flowers under his left arm in order to free up his right hand to find his keys and to unlock the door. Hearing the door open and close, Meg called from the kitchen, "Is that you?"

"I sure hope so or you're in big trouble," Nick replied amusingly.

Meg was listening to light jazz on the stereo, and there was the wonderful aroma of dinner cooking. Meg was standing with her back to him as he quietly entered the kitchen. He reached around her with the roses, lifted her soft hair to reveal her neck and placed a gentle kiss on that warm and tender spot.

"Nick, the flowers are beautiful. You gave me goose bumps."

"So I still have that old charm, huh?"

"You know what you do to me even after all of these years."

"So, you want to skip dinner? Only kidding—sort of. Dinner looks great. What's the occasion?"

"Nothing really, I just thought that it being a cool and rainy evening a nice meal of comfort food would be good. Would you please open a bottle of wine? Dinner will be on the table in about five minutes."

Meg put the roses in a vase and placed them in the center of the table while Nick opened the wine. Meg placed two beautifully presented plates, each containing a perfectly grilled salmon steak and fresh asparagus spears drizzled with a hollandaise type sauce. This was accompanied by a beautiful field greens salad. Meg lit two tall candles on either side of the roses, dimmed the dining room chandelier and then proceeded to sit at her place at the table. Nick gently and gracefully handed her a glass of wine. He sat at his place, lifted his glass to hers, and said, "Here's to our love and to the start of a great weekend."

As if being cued by the clinking of the glasses, all three cats showed up at the table to share the meal. Nick and Meg always felt that it was the civilized thing to do to share some of the dinner with the girls. There wasn't much conversation at the table as they both savored the meal and relaxed with the wine and music.

When dinner was done, Meg excused herself and left the dining room with her refilled glass of wine. Nick cleared the table, refilled his glass, and went toward the bedroom. He could see that it was dark in the room except for the flickering of candlelight.

Meg was already in bed propped up by her pillows and with the covers pulled up just far enough to reveal her bare arms and shoulders. She was sipping her wine and with her other hand patted the covers on Nick's side of the bed. Nick undressed, except for his underwear and slid into bed and under the covers next to Meg. He leaned over and gently kissed her on the lips. He could taste the wine as he ran his tongue across her now slightly parted lips. Her eyes were closed as her tongue reached out to meet his. Nick started kissing her deeply, and he could feel her fingers start to move up his inner thigh to his now, bulging and increasingly tightening shorts. He reached down and removed his shorts, freeing himself.

"Ooh baby. Looks like you're ready to go right now," Meg whispered in a sensuous but teasing tone.

"Not yet, sweetie. It's not in a hurry."

"Neither am I, baby. We got all night."

By now she was gently and slowly stroking him. Nick pulled down the covers to reveal her breasts. He dipped his fingers in his wine, rubbed it over her nipple in a circular motion and replaced his fingers with his lips. He had tasted this wine often, but he never remembered it tasting so sweet as this moment. He placed his hand on her pubic area and found her hand already there. Meg was moaning softly as he pulled the covers down to her knees and placed his head just above her hand. It really turned him on to watch her pleasure herself, so much so, that he removed her other hand so that he wouldn't finish before her. She slowly removed her hand, and Nick positioned himself over her and within seconds they both exploded in incredible pleasure.

~

Contemplating the long weekend to come, Lori decided that a quick stop at the market on the way home to purchase a bottle of wine seemed like a good idea. She had just bought a new book, and the thought of just kicking back with a nice glass of wine and a good romance novel seemed like a great plan for a girl spending the weekend alone.

The store was crowded with home goers picking up last minute weekend provisions or those picking up supplies for their very special evening activities. She tugged and released a cart from the horizontal stack corralled just outside the store entrance. She was welcomed with opened doors as she pushed the cart inside. Unfortunately, due to circumstances beyond her control, she had to go against her rule of going into a store on an empty stomach. Everything seemed to catch her eye. Just to her left upon entering was a floral display of beautiful spring flowers. Flowers always brightened up a room, so a bunch containing several varieties of daffodils, some greenery and baby's breath was picked from the tall bucket and gently placed into the baby seat part of the cart after first passing her nose. The unmarked but designed course took her next past the cheese cooler, where she picked up a nice wedge of brie and a block of white cheddar. At the end of the aisle she came to a cloth covered display table with several different bottles of wine and several small plastic cups representing each available for tasting.

Lori tasted all of them, starting with the whites and moving thru the reds. She seemed to be craving something a little on the sweet side, so she chose a bottle of the Riesling, which she thought would go well with the rather tangy taste of the cheeses that she chose. After having intended on getting just a few things, her cart was now getting rather full, so she decided to head straight for the check-out line before she incurred any more damage. She plucked a tall slender bag containing a fresh baked baguette from a wicker basket at the head of the line. The bread was still warm and the aroma started to make her mouth water. Just one more impulse buy of an imported chocolate bar as the clerk was taking the items out of her cart and she was done. A little game that she liked to play while marketing was to see what other people were buying and trying to figure out what the plans were for their dinner. Lori glanced over to the check-out counter adjacent to hers and saw a handsome young man, probably in his mid twenties, placing a box of pasta, a jar of marinara sauce, a wedge of parma, a frozen garlic bread, a bottle of red wine and a bunch of flowers. This one was a no brainer. It brought to mind the times when John would surprise her with a romantic dinner and evening to follow. Those times seemed so distant now. She found herself looking at couples demonstrating their love to one another with a mixed bag of envy and anger.

"Excuse me, ma'am?" called the check-out clerk.

Lori quickly turned her head back to her lane.

"I'm sorry. I guess I was just daydreaming."

"Did you find everything all right ma'am?"

"Uh, yeah."

The checker placed the wine bottle in a special bag and placed it into the larger shopping bag. Lori already swiped her debit card and awaited the total. She turned to look at the romantic in the next lane, but he had already gone. With receipt in hand she headed out with her two bags to her car. Within fifteen minutes she was at home and the bags were unpacked.

On her way to the bedroom to change, she turned on the radio to the lite jazz station and turned on the computer. She proceeded to the bedroom where she sat on the edge of the bed and kicked her shoes off. She dropped flat on her back on the bed with her arms outstretched over her head staring at the ceiling and enjoying the sensations of silence and relaxation. After just a few minutes the rumbling in her stomach reminded her that her reservation for a party of one was waiting. With a small grunt, she got out of bed, undressed and before putting on her favorite t-shirt and socks, she took the time to hang up her skirt and blouse. She liked the naughty feeling walking around totally nude when no one was there to see her, but only for a few minutes. After everything was put away, she slipped on her favorite dolphin shirt and a pair of socks, and went into the kitchen to get her evening of snacking and reading started. First things first, she found a vase for her flowers, trimmed the bottom inch from the stems and placed them in the water containing the special flower food that was attached to the stems. The flowers looked perfect in the middle of the dining room table. Next came the glass of wine, a large one. "What the hell, it isn't like I'm driving anywhere." She thought out loud as she lifted the glass, swirled the wine around a few times, and put it under her nose.

"Nice bouquet."

Lori cut several diagonal pieces of baguette and placed them on a large plate with the cheddar. The brie was put into the microwave just for the amount of time that it took to start melting.

"Before I settle in, I think I'll check the old e-mail and see if there is anything important on there." What she was really hoping for was an e-mail from Nick and, sure enough, she wasn't disappointed. Her heart raced as she opened it. *Man, it'll take me a week to answer all of his questions. Seems like a good thing to do tomorrow.* The rest of the e-mails were either spam or jokes from friends back home, so she closed out the session for the evening. It was still pretty warm even with the sun setting, so she brought her wine and plate of cheeses to the sun deck for some quiet time. She also brought the cordless phone since she was expecting a check-in call from John. Even though the sunset was from the other coast, it made the clouds glow with shades of red, orange, and amber. She opened the window and was immediately relaxed with the sounds of the surf and the birds foraging for their own evening snacks. The wine was already giving her a slight buzz so she thought it best to have some cheese and bread before she got too relaxed to be able to lift the knife to spread the cheese. Lori picked up her book and began to read while sipping more wine. Before long the words began to appear fuzzy. The erotic passage that she was reading made her mind drift to the thoughts of what the young man from the market was doing right now and what it would be like if Nick were here with her sharing the beautiful sunset and wine. She put the book down and just sat there listening to the music and enjoying the moment until she drifted off.

The ringing of the phone woke her. It took her a few rings before she could compose herself enough to answer. She was still feeling the buzz, but was sober enough to carry on a conversation.

"Hello."

"Lori, this is Brent. Is John there?"

"No, he's out on a project and won't be back till Sunday night or Monday. Wait a minute. Brent, you're his partner. Why didn't you know that and why aren't you with him?"

"Uh, yeah, I guess I forgot. Maybe he did mention a trip. Uh, I couldn't go this time. Lori, I'm sorry I bothered you. I'll check with him on Monday."

"Brent, where's John?"

"I think he's down in the Keys somewhere doing something with turtles. Have a good weekend."

"Thanks, Brent. Bye."

This seemed really strange. John and Brent were very close and always worked on projects together. She couldn't tell just yet if Brent was being intentionally vague or if she was still under the effects of the wine. Up until this time she really had no reason to doubt John, and maybe, she thought, there was a perfectly reasonable explanation this time. She finished what was left of the wine in her glass, picked up the plate, and headed for bed after closing the window and turning off the lamp. The chilly night air caused her to have goose bumps on her arms and legs so she quickly secured the rest of the condo for the night and quickly crawled into bed pulling the covers up to her neck. As she lay flat on her back with her eyes closed, the room slowly spun her to sleep.

CHAPTER 11

Lori was never too far from Nick's mind over the rest of the weekend and the anticipation of hearing from her again kept his heart beating at a slightly higher rate the whole time. He couldn't wait to get to the office and open his e-mail. Just seeing a message from her would at least alleviate the feeling that he had scared her off. Immediately upon arrival to work he opened his e-mail and sure enough, there was a message from dolphinlover patiently waiting to be opened.

"Hi Nick, Happy Monday. Hope you had a good weekend. You sure asked me a lot of questions, but I guess it's been a long time. I got your e-mail address from Alan back at the old station. I've been living here in Lauderdale with my husband, John. He chases mermaids for a living. Actually he is a marine biologist. What's going on with you? Soon. L"

Nick expected a much longer e-mail but was happy just to have received anything from her. He couldn't tell much from the message, but then again, Lori never was one to eagerly impart information, especially that of a personal nature. He knew that if he wanted to learn more about her he would have to be corresponding in a more personal manner. His son Adam, now a young adult, would correspond with his girlfriend back home while visiting him during the summer by using some sort of instant messaging through the computer. It was like carrying on a phone conversation only through typing. It didn't take long for Nick to find someone at work who was familiar with this concept and who was eager to explain it to him. After setting up an online account for himself complete with a user name and password, he was ready to go and hoped that Lori was open to trying it out. Excitedly, he typed a reply message to Lori.

"Lori, it was great to hear from you when I got to work today. I was wondering if you have access to computer instant messaging. I think it would be fun for us to be able to chat with each other over the computer. If you'd like to give it a try, let me know and I will give you my user name. By the way, I hope your husband doesn't catch one of the mermaids, if you know what I mean. Hope to hear from you soon. N." He hit send and immediately had the sinking feeling that the last comment about her husband may have been over the line. After all, they have barely progressed past the re-introduction phase of their new correspondences.

"Oh well, it's on its way now. Not much I can do to get it back," he muttered out loud. With that he went on with his day's work.

~

"Well, any more on the Nick and Lori story?" Pam asked as Lori hung up her jacket on the hook just inside the office door.

"There is no story."

"You mean *yet*. So what's the latest, girl?"

"He wrote me and asked a lot of questions like he wanted to know my whole story since the last day that we saw each other. I just told him that I lived here and that my husband was a marine biologist."

"And?"

"And that's it. So how was your hot weekend?"

"Well, Jorge, that's George in English for you, came over on Saturday afternoon. We had a couple of beers and a few laughs then headed south. He took me to this really hot salsa club in Miami. There was a live band and we danced and ate some great Cuban food. I just love those Cuban sandwiches with a big bowl of moros y christianos, that's black beans and rice for you gringos."

"And? I know there has to be an *and*. C'mon, at least let me live vicariously."

"And," she emphasized, "it was late, or rather early, when we got back to my place and we had a goodnight cerveza or two. I couldn't let him drive in his condition, could I?"

"I think we're getting too close to the too much information zone. I don't think I could handle the details right now."

"So, how was your quiet weekend alone?" Pam inquired.

"Well, let's see. The company was fantastic as was the food and wine. The book that I am reading gave me the best thrill that I'm going to be getting for a while, and I got a really interesting phone call."

"From whom?"

"From Brent, John's partner."

"Brent? If they are out working, why didn't John call? Did something happen to John?"

"Not yet, but that depends on his explanation. Brent called and asked for John. I thought that if John was out on a research project then why wasn't Brent with him, so I asked him. He gave me some lame excuse and seemed to step all over his tongue. All he said was that he thought that John was down in the Keys and that he couldn't go for some reason."

"OUCH! Do you think he's out screwing around on you?"

"If he's screwing anyone, it sure isn't me." Tears started welling up in Lori's eyes.

"Take it easy, baby. Before you get too upset, wait and see what he has to say. Save your energy for a fight if you have to."

Pam dabbed Lori's eyes with a tissue. "Remember, Pam is here if you need her."

"I know. Thanks."

The metal bell attached to the front door jingled the signal that there was a customer in the store. Pam went out to the front, and Lori stayed in the office and composed herself.

For the rest of the day she tried to think of what she was going to ask John and how she was going to bring the issue up when she saw him later in the evening, assuming of course that he came home today. He had not called her the entire time he had been away. Usually he called at least every other day to check in to see if everything was all right and to update her on what he was doing. She became more angry and hurt the more she thought about it.

"Pam, do you think I could leave a couple hours early today? I'm feeling pretty shitty."

"Sure thing. It's pretty slow here today. I think I can handle it myself."

"Thanks big. You're the best."

Lori walked back to the office to retrieve her jacket and purse. As she passed the sales counter on her way to the door, Pam looked up at her and said, "Good luck."

"I'll let you know how it turns out. Who knows, I may be looking for a place to sleep tonight."

Pam gave Lori a sympathetic smile as the door closed behind Lori.

When Lori arrived home, she saw that John's car was in the condo garage. Her heart started to race in anticipation of what was to come. In days long past her heart used to race for other reasons when she saw that he was home.

When she reached the third floor, she could hear the sounds of classic rock and roll coming from their condo. *Well here goes,* she said to herself as she turned the key and opened the door. John's backpack was on the floor next to the sofa, and she could see him in the bedroom. He called out, "Is that you?"

"It better be," She answered.

"I didn't think you'd be home for a couple of hours."

"Are you disappointed?" she asked.

Lori put her purse on the table, tossed her jacket over the back of the sofa and went into the bedroom where John had his suitcase on the bed and was in the process of unpacking it.

"Disappointed? Of course not. What are you talking about? Are you okay? I missed you."

"Just having a bad day, sorry. So how was your trip?"

"It went pretty well. Hit some rough seas for a while, but we got the job done."

"So, was it the usual team?"

"Yeah, why?"

"Just curious, that's all. So, what were you and Brent working on this time?"

"You sure are showing an unusual interest in what I'm doing all of a sudden."

"What do you mean? I've always been interested in what you and Brent are working on. What were you guys working on this time?"

John looked puzzled at the line of questioning and after a short pause said, "Actually, Brent wasn't with me this time. We met up with a college student when we got down there."

"Oh, is he interested in sea turtles too?"

"Sea turtles? Where did that come from? We were working on blue fin tuna migration, and it wasn't a he, if you must know."

"I was worried about you, that's all. You didn't call."

"You could have called me. I told you that I would have my cell phone on."

"I tried to call you on Saturday morning, but the message said that your service was unavailable at this time, and it transferred me over to your voice mail."

"Oh, Saturday. We were several miles out at sea, and there was no service out there."

"I left a message, and you never returned my call."

"I told you there were rough seas. My phone fell out of my bag when it got tossed around on the deck and I couldn't find it until we docked and unloaded the boat. By that time I figured that there was no use in calling you since I would be seeing you in a couple of hours." John reached into his bag and pulled out a cellophane covered rectangular box. "I brought you something from the Keys." John handed her a box of chocolate covered, key lime coconut bars. "Enjoy."

Lori took the box. She thought, *Great. He won't touch me any more because I'm so fat and now he brings me a box of candy.* Then out loud, "Thanks John. I'm sorry. I'll probably feel better in a little while. I think I need a nap." She placed the candies on the dresser top and went into the kitchen. She poured herself a glass of wine and took it back into the bedroom, took a sip, placed it on the nightstand and lay down.

John kissed her on the forehead and said, "Tell you what. You rest for a little while and I'll go out and get some Chinese for dinner. How's that? I'll get you the seafood and vegetables. I know that's your favorite."

"Sounds pretty good to me."

"I'll be back in a bit."

Lori sat up, took a long sip of the wine, and lay back down thinking that maybe she did make too big of a deal over the whole thing. The radio fell silent, and she heard the door close as John exited. She knew that he would be gone for at least an hour, so she decided that before she took a nap she would see if Nick had written her. She smiled as she saw his message appear.

"Hi Nick." began her reply. "That sounds like a good idea. My e-mail is on friendnet, and they have instant messaging. If you have the same service, we can see how it works. Just let me know what your user name is and I can look for you. Let me know when you get set up. Hope to 'chat' with you soon. L." She clicked on the send icon, logged off, and went back to bed. This time there was a smile on her face.

~

John pulled into the parking lot of the strip mall where the Chinese restaurant was located. The Chinese carry-out only took a few minutes to prepare, so he thought that he would have a cup of coffee at the coffee shop next door before he placed the dinner order. After ordering a latte, he sat down at a corner table. He took his cell phone from his inside jacket pocket and turned it on. "You have 1 message." appeared on the screen. He called his voice mail, and there indeed was a message from Lori. He listened and then deleted it before the message was completed. John took a sip of the latte and savored the coffee flavored foam. The coffee was still too hot, so he set it back down on the small round table and punched in several numbers on his phone.

"Hi baby, it's me."

"I know. I miss you a lot too. It was special for me too, Tracy—"

~

Lori felt much better after her nap and the wine. She didn't have to cook anything for dinner, which was always a good thing, and the Chinese food was pretty tasty. After dinner, Lori was feeling refreshed, so she suggested that she and John go to bed early. She was in an intimate mood and lied close to him and rubbed her hands over his body, but as usual, John said that he would love to, but right now he was pretty tired after the trip. Maybe he'd feel more like it in a day or two. He kissed her on the lips and rolled over to go to sleep. She rolled to her right side and relied once again on her book to take her to places and experiences that she could only have in her mind.

CHAPTER 12

Pam was eager to find out about how things worked out the night before. "So tell me how it went. You doin' okay today? I didn't get a call, so I guess that's a good thing, huh?"

"Everything went all right. John was there when I got home and we discussed the trip. I think I'm just being a little too paranoid."

"And how are things on the other front?"

"Nick wants to do some chatting on line instead of just e-mails. I told him that I'd give it a try. The only problem is like when will I have time to do that? By the time I get home there are a billion things to do and I would feel funny doing that with John looking over my shoulder. "

"I don't have any problem with you logging in on the office computer during your lunch break. I promise not to look over your shoulder, at least not very much. It might be fun."

"I'll have to download friendnet messaging into your computer. Is that all right?"

"Sure. Go ahead."

Lori logged into friendnet and downloaded the files. "Now, all I need is his user name and it's ready to go."

~

Nick was excited to see that Lori was open to the idea of instant messaging. He too was on friendnet, so it was just a matter of letting her know what user name to look for and to set up a time to try it out. Excitedly, he sent out reply. "Lori, I'm on friendnet too! I take my lunch break about noon. My user name is supertech. I'll be watching for ya soon! N." Nick logged on to the friendnet messaging area and quickly added Lori's user name to his contact list, which up to this time was empty. He typed d-o-l-p-h-i-n-l-o-v-e-r and clicked on the "done" icon. This highlighted her name and a notation of "off line" came up after her name. Now he was really excited. This was like a direct line to her where they could talk to each other in real time, and there would be no more waiting for e-mails.

~

"Pam, since you are in such a generous mood today, what about if I just check my daily e-mails from this computer, too?"

"Would there be any particular e-mail that you might be interested in?"

"Pam, remember, it was you that got me into this in the first place, right?"

"Guilty as charged. Now let's get back to work."

After a long day of book selling, it was time for the girls to close up the shop for the night. The lights in the front of the store were turned off, and the "closed" sign was placed on the door. Pam opened the cash drawer and took the tray into the office.

"I think I'll check my e-mail before I leave. That okay?"

"Sure hon, it'll be a few minutes before I get the night deposit ready. I'll walk out with you."

Lori logged into the friendnet e-mail, and there was a message from Nick. This was really getting to be a regular thing, and she had come to expect something from him every day. She still felt a little sneaky about it, but if this gave her something to look forward to every day, *then what's wrong with that*, she thought. There was sure damn little else to look forward to these days. Besides, it gave her a chance to use those under worked smile muscles.

"Pam, I got his user name, and he's all set up on friendnet!" Lori quickly accessed the messaging section and entered s-u-p-e-r-t-e-c-h on her contact list. The "off line" notation came up after his user name.

"You gonna try him now?"

Lori laughed.

"I don't mean it that way! I take her to one sex toy party, and now she has a filthy mind!"

"Well, it's not like I haven't thought of it, but he said that his lunch hour is around noon. Maybe I'll try and *get* him tomorrow."

"Again with the *maybe* shit. You'll do it tomorrow."

They both laughed as they left the store and lowered the gate for the night.

"You want to go get a bite before you go home?"

"No thanks, John is probably already home, so I better get home."

"Have a good night. See ya tomorrow."

"You too, Pam."

Lori was right. John was already home when she got there. *Why, she wondered, am I always in a hurry to get home when John is here, but once I get there I wonder why I was in so much of a hurry.*

John came out of the bedroom, wearing a large towel around his waist, and drying his hair with a smaller towel.

"Hey babe, what's for dinner?" was the first thing out of his mouth.

"Don't I at least get a 'How was your day?' before you ask me what's for dinner?"

"Sorry, so, how was your day?"

"Jesus Christ, John, you just don't get it, do you?"

"Get what?"

"My point exactly. Excuse me while I go get *your* dinner ready."

Lori turned sharply and went into the kitchen. She pulled a Swedish meatballs over noodles frozen dinner out of the freezer and put it into the microwave. After four minutes the timer beeped and Lori took the dinner out, pulled the cover off, and slammed it onto the dining room table. Sauce and noodles flew out and landed on John's briefcase. "Dinner is served, your highness." She said in her most sarcastic tone. With that, Lori grabbed her purse and jacket and left the condo slamming the door behind her. John just stood there looking at the mess with a look of disbelief on his face.

"What the fuck was that all about?" he asked himself out loud. John went to the kitchen counter next to the sink and pulled three sections of paper towels from the roll and wiped off his briefcase. He picked up the little plastic tray with it's remaining contents, went into the kitchen and got a fork from the drawer and a beer from the fridge, and headed for the sofa. "Well, bon appe-fuckin-teet." He said as he lifted the first meatball from the mix.

~

Lori sat in her car with her hands on the steering wheel and her forehead resting on its center. She pulled her cell phone from her purse and dialed Pam's number.

"Hello," Pam answered.

"Pam, this is Lori." She said in a quivering voice. "Is the offer for dinner still good?"

"Sure, honey. I just heated up some meatloaf and mashed potatoes. I'll set a place for you. C'mon over."

"Thanks, Pam. You got some booze over there? I could use something strong."

"Sounds like you need a visit with Dr. Cuervo. I hear that he makes house calls. See you in a few."

Lori turned off her phone and started off for Pam's.

Pam met her at the door with a juice glass full of tequila. "Here honey, something to take the edge off."

"Shit, Pam, that would take the paint off." Lori took a gulp, which was a big mistake. Her throat tightened up and she choked as she felt the liquid burn all the way down her throat.

"Easy there. I thought the meatloaf might kill you, not the tequila."

When Lori settled down and the tears cleared from her eyes, they both had a nice quiet dinner. The combination of the comfort food and Dr. Cuervo made Lori loosen up enough to pour her heart out to Pam, who was a great listener. Around nine o'clock Lori headed back home, again not knowing what to expect when she arrived.

What she found when she got there was the small tray from the frozen dinner on the coffee table with the fork still sitting inside. An empty beer bottle sat next to it. John was already in bed asleep. She quietly turned lights off, got undressed, and crawled into bed. She wasn't being courteous, she just didn't want John to wake up and restart the shit over again. She lay there for what seemed like hours before she fell asleep.

CHAPTER 13

Nick was so anxious to see if Lori was going to make contact, that he accessed the friendnet immediately after checking his business e-mails and voice mail. Of course, the "off line" notation still appeared after dolphinlover, after all, it was still pretty early in the morning. He reduced the friendnet program to a small space on his computer screen and went on with the morning's duties. The program was set up so that it gave an audible alert when someone on your contact list logged on and off. This didn't keep him from checking often throughout the morning, just in case.

~

The tequila the night before left Lori in a rather foggy state as she woke up to the sounds of John taking a shower. She had nothing to say to John after the interaction the night before, so she just laid there until she was sure that he was gone for the day. This morning there were no wishes for a good day or kiss, at least on the forehead, before John left.

Lori slowly rolled to a sitting position on the edge of the bed and fought off the residual dizziness. Once stable enough to stand, she walked toward the kitchen for her first caffeine fix off the day. As she walked past the mirror, she paused to take a look at herself. She didn't know what possessed her to do that, since she really hated looking at herself any more. But there she was, her long bed hair hanging in disarray, eyes that looked like a Lauderdale road map, a t-shirt that was so wrinkled that it made the dolphin on the front appear to be one hundred years old and socks pulled down to her ankles. "Jesus, what a mess. No wonder he doesn't want anything to do with me. I can barely stand myself." Before exiting the bedroom, she picked up the unopened box of coconut candies, looked at it for a moment and then tore off the cellophane, opened the box and took one of the individually wrapped pieces out. After one more look in the mirror, she said, "What the hell. What harm could it do to this." The candy was consumed on the way to the kitchen.

John had made a pot of coffee, so she poured herself a cup, added two teaspoons of sugar and some milk. "Goddamn! This shit tastes like motor oil!" She poured it down the sink and went into the bathroom for her shower.

The shower seemed to wash the 'stank' away, as she called it, and she began to feel a little more human. She dried off and dressed in a long skirt and long sleeved blouse, trying to cover herself up as much as possible. On her way to the door she noticed a small folded piece of newspaper on the floor near where John tossed his jacket on the sofa. Lori picked it up and unfolded it. It was a piece of a Miami newspaper and the date was last Thursday. On the other side, there was a hand written phone number starting with 786 which she recognized as a Miami area code. Under the phone number was another number, 225. It was also clear that it was not John's handwriting, but rather that more likely a woman's. She was feeling angry and foolish at the same time, as she put the piece of paper in her purse and went to work.

She couldn't wait to show Pam what she had found. All the way to work she tried to make some sense of it all. Could she still be making a big deal about nothing? Could there be a reasonable explanation for this, too? He did say that a college student met them for the project. She began to calm down a she explained away her own fears. After all, she was feeling pretty bad about herself lately and maybe she was just transferring the blame to John. Lori decided not to make a big deal of it and decided to let it go for now.

The morning at the bookshop was pretty routine. There were shelves to stock with new books, the moving of books that were not selling to the quick sale table and idle chit chat with Pam.

The time went pretty quickly, and before she knew it, it was time for lunch.

"Well, it's lunch time." Pam reminded Lori. "And you know what that means?"

"Yes, it means that one of us has to go out and pick something up," Lori answered, although she knew very well what Pam was hinting about.

"Very good. And, don't you have a little project to do on the computer?" Pam continued questioning.

"Tell you what, why don't you go and get me a tuna salad sandwich and I'll think about it," Lori bargained.

"I expect to see some action going on here when I get back," Pam said as she left the store.

Lori really wanted to log on, but for some reason still procrastinated over it. She looked at the clock and saw that if she was going to do it she only had a half hour before Nick's window of opportunity closed for the day. Pam was going to be back in a few minutes, so she had to do something fast. The computer mouse led he through the maze of programs until it came to rest on the friendnet program. Her hand shook as she opened the program, entered her user name and password. Just then Pam entered with their lunch.

"Well?" Pam asked.

Lori turned to look at her and at that moment didn't see the "on line" pop up after the contact name, supertech.

~

Nick was sitting at his desk eating one of those cup-o something or another that you just add hot water to make a thick soup. The TV across the office was on and he was watching the noon news. He was so intent on the news story that he missed the audible signal from friendnet that a contact was now on line. Glancing down at the bottom of the computer screen, he noticed that the reduced program was flashing, indicating that a contact was on line. His heart started to race, and he clumsily moved the mouse over the program to open it. There it was, dolphinlover! He immediately typed "Is that really you?" like there would be anyone else trying to contact him.

~

After taking the first bite of her sandwich, Lori heard the signal that there was an instant message waiting. "Put the goddamn sandwich down and type something!" Pam ordered. Lori's hands were really shaking now as all she could type was, "it's me." Pam saw a smile on Lori's face like she hadn't seen in an awfully long time.

"This is so great, like talking to you on the phone," appeared on her computer screen.

"It is," Lori responded.

Looking over her shoulder, Pam said "Hey, Hemingway, is that all you can come up with is two words at a time? Say something."

Nick thought that maybe this wasn't going to work as well as he thought. She wrote more in an e-mail. Maybe this will take some time until she feels more comfortable. He typed, "What are you doing right now? Are you at home?" He thought that this would require more than a two word answer from her.

"I am at work."

Pam urged her on, "Keep typing, girl."

Lori continued, "with my best friend at her bookstore on the beach."

"Whew! A breakthrough!" Pam exclaimed.

Nick replied, "That sounds really nice. I wish I was at the beach right now."

Right now Lori kind of wished he were here too. "It is pretty down here. Do you ever get down this way?"

"I have only been there once when I brought Adam, my son, to Orlando during one of his summer vacations with me."

"I remember him when he was a baby and we were at the station's Xmas party."

This brought back all sorts of images back to his mind, but he set them aside for the moment.

"Adam is all grown up now. You wouldn't recognize him. Lori, I hate to do this, but I have to go. Can we resume tomorrow?"

"This was fun," she typed. "I will look for you tomorrow about this time. K?"

"Great! Bye."

Almost immediately after typing her "bye" she saw the "on line" change to "off line" after supertech.

"Pretty cool, huh?" Pam remarked.

"I could get used to this," Lori said with a large grin. "He said that his son came to visit during the summer. Do you think that he's still married?"

"All we know is that he was. Why don't you ask him tomorrow?"

Lori thought that maybe she didn't want to know, but replied, "We'll see." She logged off and both Pam and Lori went back to bookstore stuff, both feeling happier than they did before lunch.

~

Nick felt like he was a teenager again and carried a smile on his face for the rest of the day. Even the carpool noticed that he was very different now than he was during the ride into work this morning. One of them commented, "I wonder what has him smiling so much back there?"

"Maybe it's gas," another replied. They all laughed, and Nick just kept on smiling the rest of the way home.

CHAPTER 14

When Nick arrived home, he was greeted by the smells of dinner cooking. "Hi honey." Meg greeted him from the kitchen, "Dinner will be ready in a few minutes. How was your day?"

Nick wanted to tell her but didn't know how to at the moment. Meg was a reporter and was always going for the details. He didn't feel like going into detail right now, and besides, that was a different life a long time ago in a land far away. All he could say was, "It was pretty interesting, actually. I heard from a colleague friend that I used to work with at the old station a long time ago."

"Really?" Meg called from the kitchen, "What made him contact you after all this time. Is everything all right out there?"

Nick was still in the living room going through his mail, but stopped when he heard Meg ask about *him*. Should he correct her or just let it go? He was always honest with Meg, and there wasn't any reason not to be right now. There was no reason to feel guilty, after all it was just conversation between old friends, right? He had to admit that since Lori had contacted him, the memories of that night so long ago had been brought from their resting place in the back of his mind to the forefront where it both excited him a little and made him feel uncomfortable at the same time.

"Nick, are you there?"

"Uh, yes. Why do you ask?"

"Because I just asked you if you wanted some iced tea, and you didn't answer."

"Sorry, baby, I guess I was concentrating on the mail for a minute." He glanced down to see that the piece of mail that he was staring at in his hand was an advertisement for a computer dating service. "Sure, iced tea would be great." He put the envelope down on the end table with the rest of the mail and went into the kitchen where Meg was serving up two large bowls of homemade stew, one of is favorite meals. The cats were already in position at the table, waiting for the dinner delivery. Meg handed Nick the two bowls and she picked up the two cold glasses of tea. She put the glasses at their places at the table and went into the living room and turned on some light jazz. Nick was already seated when she returned to the table. He always waited until she was seated before he began to eat.

"So, tell me about that guy's call," Meg asked as she pulled small pieces from the tender chunk of beef for the cats. Simca was next to her chair and sitting up in a very canine-like begging position. Pikabo was on the dining room chair opposite Nick with just her head visible only from the chin up, and Disa just stood by Nick's chair patiently waiting for what she was sure would be forthcoming. Meg blew on each piece to cool it before handing one to each feline diner.

"What do you want to know?" Nick asked, as he took his first mouthful.

"I suppose the first question would be, what made him contact you after such a long time?"

"I really don't know. Actually, Meg, it's a she, not a he." Nick felt better having made the correction.

"An old flame rekindled, perhaps?' Meg said with a hint of a chuckle.

"That's not funny, Meg. All I know is that she's married and living in Florida. I can only figure that something reminded her of the good old days, and she's doing an e-mail reunion of sorts. So, what have you been up to?"

"Same old, same old. Still working on that developer story. It should be done in a couple of days."

That sure went easier than I expected, Nick thought.

The cats having tasted the evening's vittles were now asleep on their respective nesting spots, and Nick and Meg having cleaned their bowls cleared the table and retired to the bedroom. Nick watched some mind numbing repeat on TV while Meg propped herself up against her pillows and worked on her project. After the yawns became two minutes apart, it was clear that it wasn't going to be too long before Nick's eyes were going to slam shut. He turned off the TV and his nightstand light, leaned over and kissed Meg goodnight.

"Goodnight, sweetheart," he whispered.

"Goodnight, honey," she returned. Then added, "Was she as good as I am?"

It was a good thing that the lights were dim because wherever that came from, it brought quite a blush to his face.

Now, more awake, Nick answered, "Meg, I really wouldn't know."

"Just curious, that's all. You know how it is, inquiring minds want to know."

With that Nick crawled across the bed and straddled her legs. "Why don't you turn out that light and remind me again how good you really are."

Meg dropped her work onto the floor and reached over and turned off her light. Nick lowered himself over her and kissed her deeply. It wasn't long before they were naked and wrapped with each other.

"Well, how was that?" Meg asked.

"Whew! It just can't get no better than that!"

"And don't you forget it," Meg warned playfully.

They kissed again and drifted off into a serene state of being and a wonderful night's sleep.

~

Lori arrived home after work feeling pretty good for a change. There was an internal feeling of happiness that she hadn't felt for a very long time. When she reached her condo door, all of the signs were present that John was already there, most prominently the classic rock music playing too loudly. Even though John was inside, it was a habit of theirs to lock the door immediately after entering. Lori searched inside her purse for her keys and found the piece of the Miami newspaper that she had put there earlier that morning. Her feelings of happiness quickly returned to the feelings of resentment and anger from earlier today. There were still the unresolved issues of the evening before. There were no words spoken between each other for almost twenty four hours and she wasn't looking forward to picking up where they left off. She took a deep breath and slowly let it out. She unlocked the door, went in and was greeted by John.

"Hey baby, what you got planned for—oh shit, I forgot that I have to ask you how your day went first. How was your day?"

"Actually, my day was really good until I realized that I had to come home to your sarcastic and white trash personality."

"Well, I see where this is going already. You sure seem to have an attitude these days. Maybe you're the one with the problem and not me."

"I'll tell you what my problem is. I have a husband that doesn't give a crap about *my* feelings any more. He is a self centered son of a bitch and all he cares about is that I have his dinner ready when he wants it."

"And that reminds me," John jumped in, "the Swedish meatballs, last night, were really a special treat. And the presentation was so beautiful."

"Shall I continue," Lori asked, "or are you not yet done with your dining review?"

"You mean there's more?" John asked.

"Yeah, maybe one last thing." Lori reached into her purse and pulled out the folded piece of newspaper. She could see John's face start to redden. "What's this all about?"

"What's what all about? Is that a coupon for a frozen dinner?"

"You bet. It's the one that I'm going to shove right up your ass. Whose numbers are these?"

"I told you, there was a student who met us at the boat. That was her number."

"And I suppose that the other number is her cabin number on the Love boat?"

"Lori, are you saying that you think I am having an affair? Why don't you just cut the bullshit and come out with it?"

"Well, are you?"

"Lori, it's tough when I have to be away from home for weeks at a time. Sometimes there are girls and we get together and have a few drinks and—"

"And screw?" Lori interrupted.

"And have a few laughs and unwind. That's all."

Lori wasn't sure that she bought into that, but deep down something wanted her to believe his explanation.

"Look, Lori, I'm sorry if I have been acting like such a shit. I've been under a lot of pressure these days, and I know I haven't been treating you like I should. I promise that I will try to do better."

"John, I feel like you've emotionally abandoned me. I could deal better with your being away on the trips if I knew that you would be here for me when you're home."

"What do you want me to do?"

"You could start by being a lot less distant and a little more intimate. Don't worry, I'm not asking that we make love every night, but maybe more than once a quarter would be a start. Do I look that bad to you that you don't have those feelings for me any more?"

"Lori, you still look okay to me."

Lori thought, *so I look okay to him. I guess that's his sorry ass attempt to make me feel better. I suppose the girls in Miami look a lot better than just okay.*

"Tell you what," John said, "Let's go out for dinner and come back here and we can go to bed early."

Lori couldn't believe what she was hearing, but she wasn't going to let an opportunity pass by. "Sure, let's go."

John even offered to drive. While on the road to the seafood restaurant of Lori's choice, John's cell phone rang. He picked it up, looked at the caller ID and sat it in the cup holder.

"Who's bothering you at this hour?" Lori questioned.

"Just a business call. I'll deal with it tomorrow."

Lori didn't know whether or not to believe him at this point, but she didn't want to jeopardize the rest of the evening by pursuing it any further. John behaved himself during dinner and actually acted like a gentleman. He even turned on the lite jazz station for the ride home.

Once back into their condo, the first words were from John. "I think that before we get into bed I'd like to take a shower."

"May I join you?"

"Sure. I'll go on in and get the water hot. C'mon in when you're ready."

Lori was pretty ready right now. It had been months since she last made love with John, and the glass of wine with dinner made her feel warm all over. She heard the water start in the shower. Lori undressed quickly and just let her clothing drop to the floor on her side of the bed. The bathroom was warm and steamy when she entered. She slid open the glass shower door and saw John washing his hair. The shampoo foam fell upon his shoulders and his body looked great. He was nicely tanned and she found the look of his wet skin very sensuous. Lori stepped into the shower and stood behind him. Her hands slightly trembled as she slowly rubbed the foam from his shoulders and continued down his back to his buttocks.

"Ooh. You're giving me goose bumps," he whispered.

This gave Lori encouragement since she wasn't sure if anything she did made him feel good any more. Feeling brave and wanting to take full advantage of the moment since she didn't know when there would be another chance, she slid her soapy hands around his waist and to his groin. It was quite apparent that he was enjoying this. "Turn around and I'll wash your back," John whispered. She loved the feeling off his hands on her body. She loved it even more when his hands moved around to her breasts. He was standing very close to her, and she could feel his excitement on her lower back.

"I think we better rinse off and get into bed," Lori said.

John rinsed off first, toweled off, and went into the bedroom. When Lori entered, he was already under the covers and had a smile on his face. She dropped the towel on the floor and walked nude over to the bed. Lori climbed in next to him and they kissed. She continued her kissing down his chest. Pulling the cover down as she continued, her kisses landed on his belly and beyond.

"Lori, unless you want it to end right now, I suggest that you come back up topside."

Lori obliged and surprised John by straddling his body and lowering herself on top of him. They both climaxed at the same time and Lori staying in position arched back and supported her body with her hands. *Oh my god* she thought, *Here comes number two.*

Lori climbed off of John and slid under the covers. They kissed. Neither one of them bothered to dress. The cool sheet felt wonderful against her now sweaty body.

"Thanks," she said to John.

"It was my pleasure," he responded. They both fell asleep, and it was only eight thirty.

CHAPTER 15

Lori had the best night's sleep that she could remember in a long time. John got up, did whatever he needed to do and left for work without even waking her. In fact, they both slept so well that neither of them heard the phone ring. The caller ID showed a call at ten seventeen. Unfortunately it was a phone number that Lori recognized from the piece of paper, a call from Miami. Lori wanted so badly to call the number to see who would answer. She picked up the handset and heard the signal that there was a message. Lori dialed the access number and heard, "Hi baby. I know that you said not to call you at home, but I was worried about you. I tried to call your cell last night, but you didn't answer. I'll try you at work tomorrow. Ciao."

There was no pleasure or satisfaction in knowing that her suspicions were more than likely a reality and she felt that there was no sense in confronting him with it right now. She needed some time to sort things out. At least now she was pretty sure that she knew what she was dealing with and that she would just do what she had to do. Maybe there was some way to use this to her advantage. Lori felt pretty bad right now, but there was at least something to look forward to later on today. She had her chat date with Nick at lunchtime. Lori couldn't wait to get to work and tell Pam what had happened. There was one more thing to do before she left for work, and that was to hit the erase message button on the answering machine.

"So, what you're telling me is that that son of a bitch is screwing you and fantasizing about some Miami bimbo at the same time?" Pam responded angrily after hearing the news.

"That's pretty much it." Lori answered.

"So, you gonna hand him his balls and a suitcase when he gets home?"

"No, I think I'm going to wait and see what I can get out of this. You know, I don't feel guilty at all any more about chatting with Nick. At least all I'm doing is talking.

In between customers, Lori and Pam had some serious heart to heart conversation. Lori had the feeling in her stomach area that something had been removed, and there was an empty hole in its place. Pam looked at her watch and said, "It's about that time. You want to see if Nick is waiting for you."

Lori wasn't sure what she wanted right now, but she shrugged her shoulders and went into the office and logged on to friendnet.

~

Nick got into the habit of logging on as part of his morning ritual. He had just returned from his favorite Italian restaurant down the street with a large meatball sub sandwich. They always put extra marinara sauce over the meatballs and extra provalone cheese on top. It was a ten napkin meal but well worth the mess. To wash it down he had a large diet soda standing by. The only thing keeping the masterpiece contained was a piece of waxed paper, which Nick slowly and carefully removed. It was quite a feat trying to accomplish this without having one or more of the meatballs escape.

Nick's mouth had just surrounded the first section of sandwich when he heard the signal telling him that dolphinlover was on line. This drew just enough attention away from what he was doing that a marinara covered meatball slid out of the side and landed in his lap. Nick set the sandwich down on a section of newspaper, wiped most of the sauce from his fingers and opened the friendnet program.

"You there?" was the message that he saw.

"It's me. You were perhaps expecting someone else?"

"Not really. How's your day?"

After a short pause, "It's all right, but it always gets better when I get a message from you. Sorry if it takes a while for me to answer, but I can only use one hand to type right now."

"Did you hurt your other hand or something?"

Nick decided to push the envelope a little and see where it went. "No, I have one hand in my lap and one on the keyboard."

Both Lori and Pam laughed when they read this. Pam said, "C'mon Lori. Time to start having fun with this. You could use a laugh right now."

Lori replied, "I didn't think I had that effect on you after all of this time. Sure is cheaper than a 900 number."

Nick liked where this was going. It was clear that Lori had a bit of a bawdy sense of humor when she warmed up. "Well, I have to do something, I have three balls in my lap."

"Wow! You're more of a man than I remembered," Lori replied.

"Well, unfortunately one of them is covered with marinara sauce."

"Kinky!"

"Not kinky, lunch. You got me so excited that I dropped a meatball in my lap." Nick wasn't sure how far he could go without going over the line, but before he could stop himself he typed, "Wish you were here to wipe the sauce off of my lap."

Lori looked at Pam with an impish smile. "Should I?"

"What the hell." Pam urged. "What do you have to lose? He's a guy. I doubt if there's anything you could say that would offend him."

Lori returned to the keyboard, smiled and typed, "How did you know that I loved the taste of Italian food."

"As much as I hate to stop here, since we are on a roll, but I have to finish the rest of my lunch and go to a meeting. Tomorrow?"

"Same time and place. Bye."

"Bye."

Lori logged off first. Nick just sat there for a minute and smiled. After eating about half of the sandwich, he went into the men's room and tried to get as much sauce off of his pants as possible. Luckily his pants were black, so it didn't show too badly. While wiping his lap he thought of what Lori had said and felt a twinge of excitement.

At about ten minutes to one, Nick picked up a reporters notebook and pen and headed out from his office towards the Production Department's conference room at the other end of the floor for what was referred to as an important meeting. Nick walked fast to catch up with Bill, the chief of Master Control, who was already halfway down the hall.

"Hey, Bill. What's *this* important meeting about?"

"I don't know. Probably someone in the front office had another brain fart and the smell is heading our way."

Both Bill and Nick entered the conference room and sat at the large oval mahogany table. Representatives from the Traffic Department, Video Tape Branch, both radio and television Broadcast Operations, and several other hangers on were already seated. The last to arrive was Leonard, the head of the television operations.

"Good afternoon. I think we all know each other so introductions are unnecessary. Let me get right to the point since everyone is busy. I have some exciting news. As you all know, television is becoming more popular every year and more and more of our foreign customers are receiving television from us and re-broadcasting it over local cable stations. We have decided to put television equipment in our field offices so that we can simulcast important news stories over TV and radio at the same time. This would also provide a remote studio in prime locations so that high level guests in those areas would be more accessible. They wouldn't have to travel all the way to D.C. to appear on our programs. The first place that we're planning to install the equipment is New York. What I need from you all is how much this is going to cost for equipment both here and in New York and how much the lines will cost to transmit this back here. Any questions? By the way, this is a priority project."

Bill raised his hand and was recognized. "All of our projects are priority these days. Is this a priority priority project or just a priority project? I suppose you need all of these figures by tomorrow, right?"

"You're close. Actually they would like them in two weeks. Any more questions?"

Nick raised his hand. "Yes, Nick?"

"Leonard, are you looking at a simple one camera operation?"

"That's all. We're planning on having a background of the skyline of New York printed and mounted on the wall behind the guest position. Just simple and quick for right now. We can expand if necessary later."

"I can get the figures for you for the basic camera set-up and associated equipment, but until I get more information, I have no idea of what type space we will be getting or what lighting will be needed. I don't suspect that it will be too complex, but unless I see some prints of the room and exactly where the set will be located, I have no idea of what I will need. For example, if the room is small, we can't use too many lights or it will get unbearably hot in there, and we can't mount them too close to the ceiling. We don't want to burn the place down. We may have to use those new fluorescents that cost more but don't produce any appreciable heat. Another issue is how we will have to mount the lights. Will we need to have some sort of a grid to mount them on? Another thing is who is going to install all of this? Do we contract it out up there or do we send our guys up there to do it?"

"Whoa! I get your point. Tell you what. Since your part is going to be more complex, I'll get your deadline pushed back a bit. In the meantime, we will send you up there to take a look around. How long do you expect that you will need?"

"Well, I think that at least two full days would work. The first day I can do some drawings of the room size and where and how the camera and lights need to be mounted. I can use the second day to make some contacts to see how much it would cost for a contractor to do the installation if it seems like something we couldn't easily handle."

"Nick, why don't you go ahead and plan a trip and do what you have to do. If there are no other questions, we can adjourn and get working on this." After a few seconds of pause, Leonard said, "Since no one jumped on me, I'll see y'all later."

With that, the room emptied as everyone went back to their respective offices. Nick was excited about the trip. It was always great to get away for any amount of time, and he hadn't been to New York in a couple of years. He thought that maybe Meg would enjoy a trip to New York. She could do some exploring and shopping while he was working and then they could have dinner together. He could even extend the trip for another day or two by adding some vacation time so he and Meg could spend some time together there. Excitedly, he called Meg to tell her about the trip.

"Hello?"

"Meg, this is Nick. How ya' doing?"

"I'm doing all right. Just busy with my assignment."

"Well, how would you like to get away for a few days go to New York? I have some work to do up there and I thought that I could stretch it out a couple of days and we could do New York together."

"That depends. When is this trip?"

"It will have to be sometime within the next two weeks. Why? You have other plans?"

"I'm afraid that I'll have to pass on this trip. I'm just about done with this assignment, and my editor just handed me another one that has a deadline in three weeks. The timing just sucks, I'm sorry. Are you terribly upset?"

"No, sweetheart, not upset, just disappointed. I understand. We can do another trip together when you get your projects done. I'll see you this evening."

"Bye, sweetheart."

"Bye, Meg."

Nick decided to get his paperwork started for the trip. He knew from experience that if he started now, there was a pretty good shot that it would be completed with all of the signatures in about a week. He also knew that no matter how early you started your paperwork, you still wouldn't have the tickets and cash advance for the trip in your hand until close of business the day before, but there was always hope.

~

Lori dreaded going home and seeing John even more today than ever before. She didn't want to hear any more of his lies or be subject to any more surprises. It took a great deal of effort for her to just unlock the door and go in. As usual, there was John standing in the kitchen opening up a can of beer.

"Hey kid, welcome home. How was your day?"

As badly as she wanted to tell him, she just said "Fine. So nice of you to ask."

"See, I'm learning. Join me in a beer?"

"No."

"What's eating you? You seem like you're pissed at something. I thought that after last night you'd be in a pretty good mood."

"I just had a pretty shitty day, that's all. I think I just want to go to bed."

"Wait. Before you go I think I have a surprise for you."

After the surprise that she found earlier this morning, she wasn't sure that she could take another one. "What surprise do you have for me today, John? Can you make it quick? I really have a headache and want to go to bed."

"Well, you know that project that I've been working on that had me travel so much?" Lori knew all too well what that project was. She just couldn't see how that could be a good surprise for her. John continued, "The Association of Marine Biologists wants me and Brent to make a presentation on our project at their convention in New York. I know that you want me to spend more time with you, so I'd like to know if you want to come up to New York with me?"

"John, that's really nice, but I have no idea what your biology project is so I would have no idea what you would be talking about."

"That's all right. I don't expect you to go to the presentation or the boring cocktail party afterwards."

Sure. Lori thought, *the lovely Miss Miami will probably be at the cocktail party, and you wouldn't want to ruin anything by having her see you with your wife.* Her thoughts continued, *then again, if I can get an all expense paid trip to New York out of this, what the hell.*

"When is this trip and for how long? I have to check with Pam and see if she can handle the shop alone while I'm gone."

"It's in a couple of weeks, and we would be gone for maybe three or four days."

"I'll think about it when my headache goes away, and I'll let you know. Nite, John."

"Does this mean no din—John caught himself amid sentence. "I'm going out for a burger or something. I'll try not to wake you when I come home."

John left and Lori got up and opened a bottle of wine. She poured herself her usual large glass and sat on the sofa. *It's amazing what a little guilt will do. All of a sudden he wants to make love and take me on a trip to New York. If it's okay with Pam, maybe I will take him up on it. At least I'll get something out of this.* She gulped down the remaining wine and went back to bed. Sleep came quickly.

CHAPTER 16

"So now the asshole wants to take you to New York? I say go, have a great time and shop till your ass falls off, at his expense, of course. I'd make him pay big!"

"And what am I going to do up there by myself at night while he's escorting Miss Miami to the ball?"

"Well, what I'd do is—"

"I think I have an idea what you'd do."

"Please let me finish. You're always cutting me off. All right, here's what I think *you* should do. You should get all dolled up in one of your new outfits that John doesn't know that he bought you yet, and head into town and find a nice classy piano bar. In a direct proportion of time to the amount of cleavage showing, some handsome prince will offer to buy you a drink and sweep you off your feet."

"And?"

"And what?"

"And the expected payoff for the drink would be?"

"Just use your imagination."

"Jesus, Pam, you have a one tracked mind. I told you that I have never been with anyone except John. I wouldn't even know how to act. I'd be so nervous that I'd probably have a heart attack, and they'd be carting me off to the nearest E.R. and leave the fine gentleman standing there holding his, uh, drink."

"Then you can sit in your hotel room wearing said dress, empty the mini bar and watch animals fuck on the Learning Channel, if that is more appealing to you. Just go and force yourself to have as much fun as possible on his dime."

"I'll think about it."

"Again with that thinking about it shit. If I didn't love you so much, I'd kick your ass. Do I have to make all of your decisions for you?"

"Yes."

"Then bon voyage, baby."

Lori had to admit that the thought of it seemed to be more appealing the more that she thought about it. She would accept John's offer when she got home tonight and get all of the details for Pam.

~

"So, how's Lori today?" started the day's friendnet exchange.

"Pretty good so far."

"I just found out yesterday afternoon that I will be going to New York in a couple of weeks for work, so our daily chats may have to be put on hold while I'm gone."

"I can't believe it. My husband just told me that he wants me to go to New York with him in a couple of weeks for some kind of conference. We may be there at the same time."

"I'll know the dates of when I'll be there in a day or so. If we're there at the same time, would you be interested in getting together for a drink, that is, if your husband doesn't have a problem with two old friends getting together."

"Pam! Come here and read this!" Lori yelled. Pam came running into the office and read the message.

"Since I'm the one making the decisions for the team," she said, "tell him YES!"

Lori paused for a moment and then typed, "Yes. That would be nice."

Nick couldn't believe what he was reading. Ever since that one evening at Lori's apartment, Nick had so badly wanted to talk to her again and maybe finally get some answers. Now he may actually get to see her face to face. He was so excited that he couldn't stay seated behind his desk. He got up and paced back and forth then sat down and typed what he thought was a straight forward yet non pressuring type of question. One thing Nick didn't want to do was to scare he off by making her feel pressured, but he was dying to find out, at least, if she remembered that night.

"Lori, I've been wondering about something for a lot of years. I promise not to bring it up again if you don't want to."

Lori looked at Pam who nodded her head and motioned toward the computer with her hand, signaling to go ahead.

"Wondering about what?" she replied.

"I've been wondering if you ever thought about that evening."

Lori knew exactly what he was talking about but decided to be coy about it.

"I've had a lot of evenings over the past umpteen years. Are you thinking of one in particular?" Lori couldn't help but feel a little excited as she too, recalled the evening in question.

"Well, actually yes. I was thinking about our, how should I put this, our unfinished symphony, so to speak."

"Well, now ya know," Pam said, "He hasn't let it go yet either. Maybe fate has brought you two together to finish this either one way or another."

Lori just sat there staring at the words on the computer screen.

"Are you gonna answer the boy, or what!?" Pam benevolently scolded.

"As a matter of fact, I have thought about it, and I really apologize. An explanation is way overdue."

Not only did this not scare Lori away, but it opened the way for possibly getting some questions answered. "Lori, I sure hope this works out. I really want to see you one more time. Since this may require a bit of coordination, could I have your phone number? It sure would make things easier. I promise not to call you and talk dirty, unless of course, you want me to."

Pam told Lori to give him the shop phone number, which she did.

"Got it. I'll call you as soon as I have the info. As soon as you have the dates of your husband's conference, let me know. My evenings will be flexible since my wife can't come with me."

When Lori heard the word wife, her heart sank and the smile left her face. "What's the matter?" Pam asked.

"I guess that answers the question about whether or not he's married."

"So? So are you. There isn't anything wrong with two friends having a drink and talking about old times, is there?"

"You're right, as usual."

Lori typed, "I guess I'll be talking to you soon."

"I can't wait to hear your voice again. Tomorrow. Bye."

Lori logged off and instead of ending with her usual smile, she had a rather concerned look on her face.

"What's wrong now?" Pam asked.

"What if we have a little too much to drink and, you know?"

"Are you afraid of what he'll do or what you'll do?"

"I guess a little of both. He's more worldly than me."

"What does that mean?"

"You know, he's had so much more experience."

"And what makes you think that?"

"He had sort of a reputation where we used to work. I heard some of the guys talking."

"Just forget all that crap, Lori. Do I have to remind you that you're an adult now and a lot more mature than you were twenty years ago, and just maybe so is he? Stop thinking like a teenage girl."

Lori smiled in acknowledgment, and they both left the office and went back to work.

Later that evening, as Lori was putting away the few things that she picked up from the market on the way home, John entered carrying a plastic sack containing a six pack of beer.

"Is that what you are planning on having for dinner or do you want me to throw an extra burger on for you?" Lori asked.

"That sounds good. I'll supply the bevs. Ya want a brewski with your burger?"

Lori didn't usually drink beer because wine got her buzz going much quicker, but since she didn't eat lunch today, the beer might be enough to get her through a dinner with John. He was already seated at the table going through the day's mail. While the burgers were sizzling on the stove, Lori tossed the loaf of bread onto the table from about five feet away. It slid into the pile of mail yet unread and a few envelopes landed on the floor.

Startled, John asked, "Was that missile aimed at me?"

"Don't worry, if I wanted to nail you with something it wouldn't be a loaf of bread, and it would have hit you. If it's not too much trouble for you, could you get the ketchup and mustard?"

John retrieved the items from the fridge and took them to the table. Lori brought over a bag of potato chips and two plates, each holding a rather large burger. John had already started his beer and hers was sitting unopened at her spot on the table. "I prefer to drink mine from a glass. Do you mind?"

John rolled his eyes as he pushed himself away from the table and got her a glass from the kitchen. "You want me to pour it for you too?"

"No thanks, John. Clearly I've already imposed upon you too much." Lori quickly poured her beer and downed it while John was still constructing his sandwich. Just as John's sandwich reached his lips, Lori asked, "Can you please slide another one over to me?"

With a puzzled look on his face, he obliged her request but before resuming his dinner he asked, "Will there be anything else?"

"No, I'm fine now," Lori said with a grin on her face. "I've decided to take you up on your offer to go with you to New York. I need the specific dates so that I can let Pam know."

"Great. I have the letter with all of the info in my briefcase." He sat his burger down on the plate and went to get the letter. "Let's see, the conference will be at the Marriott, not far from Time Square starting on Wednesday the 21st, and mine and Brent's talk will be on the last day, Friday the 23rd. We can fly in on the 20th and come back on Sunday the 25th. I figure that'll give us some touring time together on Saturday. How's that sound to ya?"

"And when is the cocktail party?"

"The party is Friday evening. You know, I told you that you didn't—"

Lori interrupted, "I know, I don't have to go to the presentation and the party because it'll be boring and all."

"It's just that it'll be a bunch of old scientists talking shop, and it could go late into the evening."

"So, none of the wives are going to be there?"

"I'm sure that some of them will be there, but you know how these parties go, after a couple of drinks the guys all get together and talk shop and the women go off and talk about all of that society shit that I know you hate."

Lori really wanted to go just to possibly catch a glimpse of Miss Miami and to make John feel uncomfortable for a while.

"It sounds like you're trying to talk me out of it. Are you?"

"No, I just know how you hate that stuff."

"Well maybe I'll just stay for a couple of free drinks and gracefully slip away. How's that?"

"That's fine with me if that's what you want to do."

"Then it's settled. I'll tell Pam."

CHAPTER 17

"I told John that I would go on the trip with him, and I think I made him nervous when I told him that I might go to the cocktail party. It was great to see him squirm a little."

"So when is this trip?" Pam asked.

"I'll need to take off from the 20th through the 23rd. That okay?"

"No problem. I can get someone to help out for a few days. So, today is the day, huh?"

"What do you mean?"

"Today you get to talk to Nick."

"Oh shit, I almost forgot about that with everything else that's going on."

"He should be calling in a couple of hours. You ready for this?"

"I don't think I have a choice, do I?"

Pam smiled at Lori and put her arm around Lori's shoulder. "You're gonna do just fine. Just think of what you have to look forward to."

"I think that right now I'm going to be sick."

Every time the phone rang, Lori's heart sank a little.

~

At about twelve fifteen Nick returned to his office. After seating himself at his desk he looked down at the phone number that Lori had given him. He reached for the phone, picked up the handset, held it up for about ten seconds and gently placed it back into the cradle. He didn't know why he craved a coffee right now, since his hands were already shaking, but he went to the cafeteria downstairs for one anyway. Maybe the walk was what he needed more than the coffee.

~

The ringing phone startled Lori out of her chair. She looked at Pam and pointed to the phone. She was afraid that her voice would be too shaky if she answered it.

"Boardwalk Books, Pam speaking. How may I help you?" Pam paused. "No, we're located one block south of the Baskin Robbins. You're welcome." Pam hung up the phone. "Sorry hon, false alarm."

Almost immediately the phone rang again. Lori looked at the clock. It was twelve thirty. Pam answered the phone. "Boardwalk Books, Pam speaking, how may I help you?" After not more than five seconds of silence, Pam said, "One second please." She held the phone out to Lori, who was standing next to her. "It's for you."

"This is Lori," She said nervously.

"My god, it's so good to hear your voice. I can't believe it's really you."

"Oh, it's really me, all right, and I'm nervous as hell right now."

"And you think I'm not? I was up to shaking speed even without the coffee that I just drank. So, did you find out any more about your trip?"

By now they were both much more relaxed about talking to one another. It felt as if they had been talking all along.

"Yes, I talked to the assho—I mean John last night and it looks like I'll be in the Big Apple from the 21st through the 24th. I may be free on Friday evening, the 23rd."

"Oh man, I still can't believe it. As soon as I hang up I'm going to the travel office and set up the trip."

"I may have something going for a couple of hours on Friday evening, but I will be free for a while after that. Is that a problem?"

"Lori, whatever time you have will be great with me. I'll call you as soon as my plans are set in stone. You sound great, Lori."

"You too, Nick. Talk to you soon."

"You bet! Bye."

They both hung up at the same time. Lori looked at Pam and beamed. "Looks like I have a date. I'll know for sure maybe tomorrow."

~

Nick immediately went to the travel office and arranged for his trip. He would be leaving Washington on Thursday the 22nd taking the seven o'clock train and returning on Saturday the 24th. The travel office booked him at the La Quinta hotel, not far from the train station and a short subway ride to the New York Bureau. While at the travel office he picked up a map of Manhattan. He couldn't wait to tell Lori, so he took a chance that she was still at work and called her.

"Good afternoon. Boardwalk Books, Lori speaking." She waved at Pam to get her attention, then pointed to the phone and mouthed silently, "I think it's Nick."

"Hello, it's me again. Well, I have my plans made, and it looks like Friday evening is a go."

"That sounds great. I can hardly wait," Lori said, trying not to sound too excited.

"I'll be staying at the La Quinta near the train station. Where will you be staying?"

"We'll be at the Marriott near Time Square. I've never been to New York so I have no idea where that is in relation to anything."

"I have a map here, let's see, looks like you're staying just a short cab ride away from me. I'll be in my hotel room after four on Friday, so just call me there and let me know when you'll be free. In the meantime I'll find a nice quiet place for us to meet, and we can talk over old times and have a drink or two. That sound okay with you?"

"Sounds like a plan to me. I'll call you then, and I guess I'll be seeing you in a couple of weeks."

"Looking forward to it. Have a good evening, Lori."

"You too. Bye."

Lori placed the phone in the cradle and looked up at Pam, who was anxiously awaiting to hear what had just transpired. "Two calls in one day? When things start moving they really move quickly, don't they? So, what gives?"

"He told me where he was staying and that he would find a nice quiet place for us to have a couple of drinks and talk over old times."

"See, you already had him drooling all over you like a horny school boy and all he's talking about is a quiet place to talk and have a drink or two."

"I know," Lori replied in a sing-song sort of whine.

"You almost sound disappointed that there isn't more to it."

"Well, as Yogi Berra used to say, 'It ain't over till it's over.'"

"I can see that you're going to be a basket case around here for the next two weeks. What you need to concentrate on for now is to not piss John off to where he cancels you out of the trip."

"I'll be a very good girl. I promise."

CHAPTER 18

"Lori, wake up," John said closely to her ear as he gently shook her shoulder. "We gotta' get going. The cab will be here in an hour."

Lori slowly pried her eyes open and squinted at the digital clock. It rudely glared back 5:00 in bright red. "Why in the hell did you have to get such an early flight?" she asked groggily. Normally Lori had no trouble getting up at this hour when it was for watching a sunrise, but today was particularly difficult. She knew that she was going to have a problem in getting to sleep the night before. The excitement in knowing that she was going to be seeing Nick soon and the anger and resentment that she was feeling toward John right now created a cyclone of mental activity that was greatly attenuated by a large dose of Chardonnay. John was in the kitchen and either didn't hear her or just chose to ignore the whining. Lori pushed herself up to a sitting position on the edge of the bed. In the process of removing her t-shirt and just at the point where she was naked from the neck down and it covered her entire head, John came in with a cup of coffee for her.

"That really is a sexy look for you, and I appreciate your trying to seduce me so early in the day, but we really have to get going," John said in a boyish tone.

All Lori could think of to say right now was a fuck you, so she decided that the best course of action would be to gracefully accept the cup of coffee and just say, "Thanks. I'll be ready when the cab gets here."

John was used to traveling, so he had everything packed the night before except his oral hygiene items and shaving equipment. The only difference this time was that he had packed his suit, tie and good shoes. Lori had taken her shower the night before, so all she had to do was comb out her bed hair, brush her teeth, and to pack her few necessities. Her plan was to buy an outfit to wear to the party once she got to New York. At about ten minutes until six, both John and

Lori rolled their suitcases to the elevator and down to the street to wait for the cab. As promised, the cab arrived on time, and within an hour they were at the airport.

The check-in went smoothly and the departure monitor showed that flight number 617 to New York, LaGuardia Airport, was scheduled to depart on time at 8:15 from gate four. There was enough time to stop at the coffee shop and get a little something to eat.

"What'll you have?" John asked. Normally just a cup of coffee would suffice, but since today was the start of, John's Going to Pay Through the Ass Week, Lori decided to go all out. Besides, Lori was starting to get a headache from not eating and still felt a little hung over.

"I'll have a venti mocha latte and," Lori pointed, "that piece of carrot cake over there."

"Well, isn't she the hungry one today. I'll just have a grande coffee of the day. Please leave room for milk," John ordered.

Lori thought, *he thinks I'm hungry now? He ain't seen nothing yet!* They took their orders to a small café table and sat down. While her coffee cooled enough to drink she searched through her purse to find a couple of ibuprofen. During her search she saw the paper with the information about where Nick was staying. This brought a smile to her face and made her feel a lot better. It was a good thing that John was so engrossed into his newspaper, because her mind was wandering to any number of places other than the right here and now. If he had any intention of carrying on a conversation with her she probably wouldn't have any idea of what he was saying anyway. It didn't seem like any time at all before the gate agent picked up the gate microphone and announced the boarding call.

"Well, I guess that's us," John said as he folded up his newspaper.

"Huh, oh, I guess I was doing a little daydreaming." Lori picked up her purse and half full container of coffee. She closely followed John across the corridor and one gate down to gate four. They were one of the first to board after the special needs folks and the first class passengers since their seats were near the rear of the plane. Lori slid across to the window seat, pulled the plastic window shade down and buckled herself in for the ride. Before long the plane was in the air, and she was asleep for the duration.

~

In less than three hours they were in New York standing in a four person thick line around the baggage carrousel. The noise was deafening to Lori and soon her headache returned. One of the first things she noticed about New York was the much quicker pace and rudeness of the people. Arms were coming in from behind, grabbing a suitcase and pulling it through, forcing a space to open between the people that immediately refilled with more humanity. Lori was starting to feel claustrophobic, but there was no way she was going to retreat and get lost in the crowd. She thanked god as she saw her suitcase come through the small opening between the tarmac and the inside. As she reached for her suitcase, she saw John's arm reach past her grabbing it and sharply pulling it off of the conveyor. As soon as his bag emerged, he grabbed it with his free hand and said loudly to Lori, "Grab my belt and don't let go. I'm gonna' see if I still have those old football moves." Lori held tight to his belt, closed her eyes, and allowed John to pull her and the suitcases through the line and to a relatively clear space where they caught their breath and laughed. "Now the real fun begins. We get to take a New York cab ride to our hotel. You want to stop at the bar first?"

All Lori wanted to do was to get to the hotel and lie down. "No thanks," she said, "Let's just get this over with."

It wasn't too far to where the cabs were lined up and as soon as their turn came, the cabbie tossed the luggage into the trunk and slammed the trunk lid shut. Lori and John were already in the back seat when the driver got in, turned to them in the back seat and said, "Where youz guys goin'?"

Lori couldn't help but smile since this was exactly then way that she had seen it on TV. John answered, "We're going to the Marriott near Time Square."

The cabbie started the meter, and the cab lurched from the curb and into the river of other cars going into town. Their eyes were wide opened as the cab was maneuvered into any space barely large enough for it to fit. They were amazed that as packed as the roads were, the cab actually continued to move through the mass. Perhaps it was the frequent front seat mantras of "get the fuck ovah" or "move the fuck outta my way if you don't know how to drive" that made the path miraculously clear. From nowhere a fire truck emerged behind them and as if by Star Trek style transporting, suddenly reappeared in front. *New York was truly a magical place*, Lori thought. Suddenly, a police car that was immediately in front of them turned on the flashing light and stopped, triple parking in front of a sandwich shop. As the officers exited from either side, the cab driver leaned across the front seat and yelled out of the window, "What the fuck you doin? You drive like you're a bunch of fuckin' tourists!" The officers waved him off as he turned sharply into the next lane over to the left.

At last the cab came to rest in front of the Marriott. John paid the driver who gave John a receipt and unloaded the luggage. As soon as their seats were vacated, another passenger with a suitcase entered the cab and told the cabbie that he was going to the airport. Thus is a circle of life in New York City. The bellman loaded their bags onto a small cart and wheeled it into the hotel where they proceeded to register and follow the bellman to their room. The bellman gave them a short tour of their suite, which earned him a tip. John went to look out of the window while Lori just collapsed with exhaustion onto the bed face down with her arms and legs spread. The insulated windows kept most of the city's noise outside, which was a good thing.

"We passed a diner a few blocks away. You hungry?" John asked.

"As a matter of fact I am," Lori replied. "Let's go."

The diner was just finishing the lunch rush so there wasn't too long of a wait before they were seated. The waitress, dressed in typical diner attire placed menus in front of them and took their drink orders. Lori and John both lowered their menus at the same time and looked at each other in amazement.

"Is this for real?" Lori asked. "A cheeseburger platter costs eleven dollars?"

"You ain't in Kansas any more," John replied. "Don't worry about it. They gave me some expense money. Just enjoy it."

Oh, I'm going to enjoy this, all right. If you only knew, Lori thought. "Here's to New York," she said as she lifted her iced tea glass and clinked a salute to John's.

"Indeed," he replied.

CHAPTER 19

Since Nick was scheduled on today's seven o'clock train, he needed to get up at approximately four thirty. He didn't know how it worked, but whenever he needed to get up at a time other than the usual, his internal alarm clock always woke him up about ten minutes before the alarm went off. There was always the feline back-up system to fall back on. If he told the girls the night before, what time he needed to get up, they were right there, doing their morning paw massage on his chest or lower, which was affectionately known as the bladder dance. The only quicker way to wake him up was one of the girls getting ready to wharf up a hairball on the bed. As quiet and least disruptive as possible, he slid out from under the covers and got out of bed. Unfortunately, that wasn't enough to keep from awakening Meg.

"Good morning sweetie," she said after a yawn and a stretch. "You want me to make you some coffee?"

"No thanks. You can go back to sleep. I'll take care of the girls and maybe they'll let you sleep in. I'll kiss you good-bye before I leave the house."

"Okay," she replied while pulling the covers back up to her neck.

The first order of business was to feed the girls and clean the litter boxes. His bag was already packed, so all he needed to do was take a shower and brush his teeth. He would get a coffee at one of the shops at Union Station. After checking to make sure that he had all of the information that he needed from the office in his brief case, he went into the bedroom, leaned over and kissed Meg gently on the lips.

With her eyes still closed, she smiled and said, "Have a good and safe trip."

"I will. I promise that I'll call you every day, even though I'll only be gone for two nights. I told the girls to take care of you while I'm gone."

"I love you, Nick"

"I love you too, Meg." Nick gave her another kiss and closed the door most of the way. He decided that since this was such a short trip he would just drive to the train station and leave his car there. There was little traffic to be concerned about at five thirty, so by the time he parked the car and confirmed his reservation, he still had almost an hour to get a breakfast sandwich and coffee at a fast food restaurant before boarding.

About fifteen minutes before departure he boarded the train, put his bag on the overhead rack and settled in by the window. It was going to be about a three hour ride to New York, where he would be getting off at Penn Station, right next to Madison Square Gardens. The train left Union Station and proceeded north through a not so beautiful part of D.C. As he stared at the passing scenery, he thought about what he needed to do when he got there, but mostly the fact that in less than forty-eight hours he would be seeing Lori. He knew that he had certainly changed over the past two decades, both physically and emotionally, and wondered how the years had treated Lori. It really didn't matter, yet he was still quite nervous about their meeting.

The train made several stops along the way, like Wilmington, and Philadelphia. Soon the train clacked its way through New Jersey and into New York, where it terminated at Penn Station. Nick pulled his bag down from the overhead and exited the train. The escalator carried him to the main floor of the station where, not unlike Union Station, there were lots of shops and news stands. One thing that he really enjoyed about New York City was the fresh baked bagels. Directly in front of him was a bagel shop, and having no will power when it came to such things, he ordered half dozen assorted bagels for the road. Second order of business was to call the Bureau on the company provided cell phone and announce his arrival.

"G.N.N. New York News Bureau, Nat speaking." Nat was the New York Bureau Chief.

"Hello Nat, this is Nick from D.C."

"Good morning. We've been expecting you. Where are you?"

"I'm at the train station, ready to head your way."

"Great. You are only about fifteen minutes away, traffic permitting. We'll have a pot of fresh Soho coffee waiting for you."

"Sounds great. I already have the bagels. See you in a few."

"You bet. Bye."

Nick hailed a cab and headed directly to the Bureau. Shortly thereafter he was standing in front of an enormous building. G.N.N. leased space on the twenty-third floor. The elevator door opened and right in front of him was a door that said "G.N.N. New York Bureau." He opened the door and entered. There was a receptionist seated in a small area with several comfortable chairs and a television set.

"I'm here to see Nat. He's expecting me."

Before the receptionist could ring Nat, Nat saw Nick through the glass and waved. Nat opened the door to the main area and welcomed Nick in with a handshake. "Good to see ya. C'mon back."

"Good to be here."

Nat led Nick to his corner office, which had a great view of the city and the Statue of Liberty. "You can leave your bag in here while I show you around."

"Thanks."

Nat first took Nick to the office kitchen area. "Make yourself a cup of coffee and I'll start the tour. Where's the bagels?"

"You can't smell the onion and garlic through the bag?"

"Got an everything in there?"

Nick opened the bag and Nat took a still warm bagel out of the bag. He held it up and said, "Thanks!"

Nick took out an onion bagel, rolled up the bag, sat it on the counter, and followed Nat with his coffee and bagel.

"I'll give you a little tour, then I'll turn you loose to do whatever you need to do. If you need me for anything, just call me. I think you'll find for the most part, everyone will cooperate with you. There are still a few old radio guys around that hate the thought of TV coming in here, but I don't think they'll bother you." They walked into an open office area with a few cubicles. "This is where the writers and editors hang out, and over there is the small radio studio where we do live cut-ins during the programs from D.C." Nat next took him to a small room that used to be an office. "Here's your studio, Nick. Not much room, but I guess you guys will do some magic. I told Leonard that the space was pretty small, and he said that you could make it work."

"Believe it or not, with the new small cameras and new cool, low wattage lights that are available, I think we can get some TV out of here. Let me do some snooping and some measurements and I'll let you know what I come up with."

"Like I said, if you need anything, just ask. Outside of that, I'll leave you alone."

"I appreciate that. Thanks. Oh, there is one thing. I could use a small ladder."

"I'll have one brought in."

"Thanks."

Nat walked out of the room and left Nick standing alone in the middle of the room. He took a 360 degree look around. The ceiling was suspended and pretty low for TV lights, but he needed the ladder to see how high the real ceiling was with the acoustical tiles removed. The air conditioning to the room would probably need to be beefed up a bit, and he needed to check to see if there was enough amperage to the room. To avoid long extension cord runs there needed to be some electrical quad boxes installed closer to the ceiling near where the lights would be installed. Nick took lots of detailed notes and decided that he would wait until after lunch to see what was above the ceiling tiles. He left his notes and briefcase in the room and headed out in search of the perfect corned beef sandwich and a Dr. Brown's soda.

~

Lori had no idea what time it was, but she could see that the sun was up and so was John. As she leaned over to John's side of the bed where the digital clock was, she heard the sound of a key in the door. The door opened and she could see John backing in, pushing the door opened with his rear end. In his hands were two large containers of coffee and on top of each lid sat a muffin of some sort. She looked back at the clock and saw that it was 7:45. Lori took the stack from John, and he sat his down on the nightstand next to the clock. The muffin appeared to be banana nut and the coffee smelled pretty good, so it didn't take long for them both to be into their breakfast.

"So, what did this gourmet breakfast cost, about fifteen dollars?" Lori half seriously asked.

"Believe it or not, it was free. There's a complimentary breakfast bar in the room off of the lobby. I thought this would hold you for a while."

Lori took a long sip of the coffee and asked, "So what time did you get up? It's only seven forty five, and you're all dressed and ready to go."

"I got up about six thirty. I had to check and see what sessions I needed to go to today and make a couple of calls. I wanted to see if Brent was here yet."

Lori bet that she knew to whom one of the calls was made. She almost forgot that the real reason for this trip was for John's work. "So, what time do you have to be in school?"

"The first session is at nine. There are several of them today, so I'll probably be tied up until at least four thirty."

"What about lunch?"

"I'll probably have to have lunch with the group. You know, they'll want to talk shop and all."

"So, you gonna give me some lunch money, or what?"

John looked into his wallet and pulled out a twenty and held it out to her. "Here you go."

"Nice start, Diamond Jim. What if I want more than a cheeseburger? I may want to treat myself to an afternoon snack. How about another twenty?" John pulled out another twenty and handed it to her. "While you have the safe open, remember, I have to go out and buy something pretty for the cocktail party. You want to be proud of me, don't you?"

John painfully handed her his American Express card. "Lori, you don't have to go crazy, now. Before I go, you want a pint or two of blood, too?"

"Maybe later," she said with a smile. "So, is he here?"

"Is who here?"

"Your partner in crime, Brent. Have the exhaust fumes gotten to you already?"

"Yes, he's here, as a matter of fact. He got in late last night."

"Well, be sure and tell him that I said hi and that I'll see him Friday evening."

"Yeah, sure."

John finished his coffee and muffin and went into the bathroom to take a shower. Lori took her container of coffee with her over to the window, pulled back the curtains and looked outside. As she looked out at all of the buildings, she couldn't help wondering if Nick was already in town and if so, how near he might be right now and what he might be doing. Her thoughts were interrupted by John coming out of the bathroom wearing one towel around his waist and the other over his shoulder like a toga. She knew that there were only two bath towels in the bathroom, and John was using both of them. This was so typical of John, only thinking of himself.

"Before you leave, call the desk and order me a couple of towels."

"What for?"

"You're the scientist here, do the math. You have two dry bath towels, you get two wet, now how many dry towels does that leave?"

"I saw more towels in there, Lori."

"You saw hand towels, Einstein. Get it? Just order me two towels. It's really simple."

"All right, just get off my shit, will ya? I promise not to use *your* towel any more. Okay?"

John went to the phone, dialed the desk and ordered two more towels for their room. "Happy now?"

"Thank you, John," Lori said sweetly

John finished getting dressed and combed his hair. "Well, I'm out of here. Have a good day and I'll see you later. We can go out and do dinner."

"Let's see how tired I am after a hard day of shopping."

John just shook his head and left the room. The door barely closed when there was a knock on the door. Lori opened the door and took the two towels from the maid and went into the bathroom for a leisurely shower, after which she donned the very soft robe that the hotel graciously provided. Before she ventured out into the city, Lori took advantage of the peace and quiet by curling up into one of the over stuffed chairs and reading a few chapters of the book that she brought with her. The time went by quickly, and it was already nearly eleven o'clock.

Feeling refreshed and ready to go, Lori dressed and checked to make sure that she had the proper ammunition for her safari into the jungle of the city. She picked up the cash with one hand and the credit card in the other. Looking at each she remarked to herself, *See, you can have them both. I have paper and I have plastic. Time to press on.* She was getting pretty hungry, so her first mission was to find some provisions.

~

Nick knocked gently on the doorframe of Nat's office to get his attention. Nat looked up from the computer keyboard. "What can I do for ya?"

"I'm going to get some lunch and was wondering where you suggest I could go for a good corned beef sandwich."

"That's easy. There's a deli a couple of blocks from here. When you leave the building, turn left. Go two blocks down and make a right. It will be right on the corner. Can't miss it."

"Thanks. I'll be back in a bit."

"The ladder should be in the room when you get back. Enjoy."

Nat returned to his typing and Nick followed Nat's directions to find Moe's, exactly where Nat said it would be. It was still a little early for the lunch rush, so there was no seating problem. The waitress seated him at a small table by the window, and in less than thirty seconds there were two metal bowls, one with pickles and the other with fresh home made sauerkraut, placed on the table in front of him. He already knew that he was going to like this. While munching on the crisp pickle, he looked at the deli counter where a rather rotund man wearing a white apron and an ice cream hat was cutting slices of fresh corned beef from a large brisket on an automatic meat slicer. The cooler case contained equally large pastramis, varieties of smoked fishes, sausages and lots of other items that were making his mouth water. The waitress returned and asked, "What'll you have today?"

"I don't know; I haven't seen a menu yet."

"Honey, there ain't no menu." With her thumb she pointed over her shoulder to the deli counter. "What you see is what we got."

"All right, I'll have a corned beef on rye with brown mustard and Swiss."

"Nope, no cheese. You want that corned beef hot and through the garden?"

"Why no Swiss? I see it in the case over there, and what does through the garden mean?"

"This is a Kosher deli and that means no milk with the meat. You want goyisha, go to McDonalds. Through the garden is with lettuce and tomato."

"Got it. I'll have a hot corned beef on rye, through the garden and with brown mustard."

"You want fries or potato pancakes with that?"

"I'll have the potato pancakes, please, and oh yeah, a cream soda if you have it."

"Comin' right up."

The waitress yelled his order across the floor to the deli man, who immediately started assembling the order. The slicer moved back and forth across the brisket until there was a large mound of corned beef on a piece of waxed paper. The plate arrived with a huge sandwich, two large potato pancakes and a small container of applesauce. The waitress brought a glass of ice and a can of cream soda. It was a lunch to die for. Finishing everything but half of one of the potato pancakes, he asked for the check.

"No check, just go up to the counter," the waitress instructed. At the end of the counter, near the window was an old fashioned cash register. The deli man met him there and asked, "What did you have?"

"I had a corned beef sandwich, soda and potato pancakes."

"Six fifty," the deli man said almost immediately.

Nick gave him a ten. The deli man gave him his change and said, "Thanks and Shalom."

"You're welcome," Nick responded and left a two dollar tip on the table before returning to work.

~

Lori walked about three blocks before she found a café that had outdoor seating with umbrellas. It was a beautiful day, and she really enjoyed watching the busy New Yorkers as they walked past. They sure looked different from what she was used to seeing on the beach. Lori sat down at one of the round tables and picked up the menu. Before long a young man in a white shirt, black slacks and a black bow tie came to her table.

"May I get you something to drink while you look over the menu?"

"Thanks, I'll have a glass of your house white wine please."

"Very good," he said with a nod.

Everything looked really good, and expensive, but since money was no object, at least for a few days, what the heck. The waiter returned with her wine and placed the glass on a small white napkin. "May I take your order?"

"Yes, please. I think I'd like to start with the French onion soup and then I'd like the grilled salmon salad."

"Excellent," he replied as he wrote the order on his little pad. "I will be right back with your bread."

Lori sat quietly sipping her wine and observing the city sights when she heard a familiar voice. "Lori? Is that you?"

She turned and was surprised to see Brent standing beside her. "My god, Brent, what are you doing here?"

Looking puzzled, he replied, "I'm here for the same reason you and John are, the conference. What a pleasant surprise."

"No, I knew you were here for the conference, I mean why aren't you at the conference now?"

"They gave us an hour and a half free time between sessions. Would I be imposing if I joined you for lunch?"

"No, please sit down. John said that you all would be having lunch together and talking shop."

"A few of them are, but most of the group went off with their spouses or significant others to explore and get some fresh air. I thought John called you after the session and was meeting you for lunch. Obviously I was mistaken."

The waiter arrived with the bread and butter and asked Brent if he could get him something. Brent ordered a glass of Merlot and a turkey sandwich on a small baguette and a side of orzo salad.

"So, what are your plans for this afternoon?" Brent asked.

"I'm planning on doing some shopping and get something nice to wear for the party."

"I'm glad you changed your mind and are coming. John said that you didn't want to come to the party."

"Actually, Brent, it was John that was trying to convince me that it was going to be too boring for me."

The waiter brought Brent's wine and Lori's soup. Brent lifted his glass, and Lori lifted hers. "Here's to a beautiful day and a beautiful lady," Brent toasted. They touched glasses and took a drink.

Lori always enjoyed being in the presence of Brent. He was a handsome man, fit and a real gentleman, pretty much the opposite of John. From the first time that they were introduced, Lori felt somewhat of an attraction to him, and had a feeling that it might be mutual. Brent was single and would be quite a catch, but he never seemed to want to settle down and do the family thing.

"That was very sweet. Thank you," she said, feeling a slight blush come over her.

The waiter brought both Lori's salad and Brent's sandwich. It was a good thing that the food had arrived since she was beginning to feel the effects of the wine. She had often wanted to ask Brent if he knew anything about John and Miss Miami, but never had the courage. She took one more gulp of the wine and out it came.

"Brent, is John screwing around on me?"

Brent had just taken a large bite of his sandwich and almost choked on it when those words hit him. He managed to swallow what he had in his mouth and washed it down with some wine. This also gave him a moment to think.

"Lori, it's really not my place to get in the middle of something like this. What makes you think that anyway?"

"There were some things that made me suspicious, like when you called asking for John when he was away on a project, then I found a piece of paper with a phone number and some other number like a room number on it. He explained those things away, but I just had a bad feeling. Then there was a message on the answering machine from woman in Miami who sounded a little more friendly than just a business associate. Besides that, he hasn't wanted to be very close to me for quite a while, if you know what I mean. Then there's the cocktail party issue. Is she going to be there?"

"Lori, he hasn't confided in me about having an affair. I have to admit that I could never understand why someone would want to do that when he had such an incredibly beautiful and sensuous woman waiting for him at home. As for the last trip, I couldn't go because I had some family business that I needed to take care of. I knew that the group was meeting a student intern down there to help out. I was sitting at my parent's house and doing some work and I just forgot that they already left for the trip. That's when I called you. I have noticed that John has been acting like a teenaged boy lately, and I've had to get his attention and try to get him to focus on what we're doing. Sorry I can't help you more. Is there anything you want me to do?"

"Can you just be there if I need someone to talk to?"

Brent took her hand into his and said, "I can be there for anything you want."

Lori hoped that he really meant that. She smiled warmly. "I may take you up on that sometime. Let's eat. I have some serious shopping to do, and you have to get back to work."

They finished their lunch and the check arrived. Brent quickly grabbed the check. "This is on me," he said.

"Thanks. Next one is on me?"

"Indeed," he said with a smile. They both got up from their seats. Brent came over to Lori and gave her a close hug before they headed off in different directions.

~

Nick returned to the Bureau, and checked in with Nat immediately upon his return. "Nat, I just wanted to let you know that I'm back. Also, I'm going to have to get over to the La Quinta and check in. I think check in is about four o'clock."

"No problem. Let me know when you're ready to go, and I'll see if we can get you a ride."

"That'd be great. I may not be too much longer here."

Nick went back to the room and as promised there was a small ladder standing in the middle of the room. Nick climbed to where he could reach and removed one of the tiles. He could see that there was another seven inches of space to a concrete ceiling. He made notes about lighting possibilities and after looking around decided that the best place for the background picture would be on the shorter wall on the north side of the room. Next he headed off to find the building manager to discuss the addition of the quad boxes, the possibility of drilling into the concrete ceiling and the air conditioning. After what Nick felt was a very productive day, he went back to Nat's office.

"Well, I've done all the damage that I can think of today. There's a small chance that I may have to come back for a final look tomorrow, but as far as I'm concerned I have all the info that I need right now. If that offer for a ride is still good, I think I'll take you up on it."

"Sure thing," Nat made a quick call and said, "There will be a black Suburban out front in five minutes."

"Thanks for your hospitality, Nat. I'm sure we will be in touch soon."

"My pleasure. Don't forget your bagels."

Nick picked up his suitcase, retrieved his bagels from the kitchenette and headed downstairs where, sure enough, there was a ride waiting for him.

Nick was pretty tired and very happy to be checked into his room. Since he had such a large lunch, he doubted if he was going to eat dinner, but a walk and a dessert before bed might be a nice way to unwind. Tomorrow was going to be something special and he wanted to be at his best, so it was most likely going to be an early evening. Before taking a short power nap, Nick called Meg.

"Hello," Meg answered.

"Hi sweetie, I just wanted to let you know that I'm here and all checked in. Everything okay out there?"

"It's good to hear your voice. Yes, everything is all right I've just been busy finishing up my project so that I can meet the deadline. The girls and I miss you already."

"I had a long and busy day too, so I'm going to crash out early. I love you and please tell the girls that I said hello and send my love."

"I sure will. I love you too. Talk to you tomorrow."

"Sleep well. Bye."

Nick hung up the phone, rolled over on the bed and fell asleep.

~

Lori was feeling pretty good right now as she looked over her day's catch. After lunch with Brent she walked a few more blocks and found a woman's clothing store whose front window display seemed to beckon her. There were dresses, blouses, shoes, and some great accessories. There were no prices visible from the window, but the fact that there was a greeter at the front door wearing a tuxedo gave her a hint. He held the door opened for her and half bowed as she walked in. Immediately, a sales associate greeted her and offered her a cup of tea, which Lori graciously accepted. *This was going to be fun*, Lori thought. *John may fail to see the humor in it, but that's too bad.* After trying on several dresses and shoes, she decided to take a beautiful but simple strapless black dress, which revealed some cleavage, matching heels and a fringed shawl. Wanting to spread the wealth around the city, she stopped at another store where she bought some gold hanging earrings, a simple but elegant necklace and a small purse with a gold chain strap. Total value of this deal was close to three thousand dollars. Pam would most certainly be proud of her right now. Lori was going to let the mailman surprise John with the bill after they got home. She put everything in the closet and waited for John to return from the conference and take her out to a fabulous steak dinner at a restaurant that she passed along her journey.

CHAPTER 20

The day that Nick had been waiting for, for almost twenty years was finally here. There hadn't been any contact with Lori for a while, so he hoped that everything was still a go for their meeting this evening. He was so nervous that he couldn't eat breakfast. He had to find something to do to keep his mind occupied for the rest of the day until, or if, she called. He still needed to find a nice quiet place for them to meet, so after showering and dressing he went to the front lobby where the concierge had a small desk.

"Can I help you with something?" the concierge asked.

"Yes. I'm looking for a nice quiet place where I can meet someone and have a few drinks and talk."

"We have lots of places like that around here. Where in town are you interested in finding such a place?"

"Somewhere between the Marriott and here would be perfect."

"There's the Whispering Wind lounge about seven blocks from here. It's got great atmosphere, casual, good drinks and on Friday nights they have live music."

"That sounds pretty good. What's the address? I have time to kill, I'll take a walk and check it out."

"Actually I have one of their cards here. Give them this card and the first drink is on the house. There's a map on the back. We're right here," the concierge said as he drew a small circle on the map. "Hope you have a great time."

"Me too, thanks."

Nicks strolled down the streets toward the Whispering Wind while thinking of all of the questions that he wanted to ask Lori. Then the thought occurred to him that maybe it was time to just let it go and forget it. What happened just happened. They were both in very different places in their lives back then. Wouldn't it be nice to just pick up where they left off and be friends. If she wanted to talk about it, then okay, but he wasn't going to bring it up. He felt better having come to a decision.

The Whispering Wind wasn't opened yet, but from the looks of the place it seemed like what he was looking for. He only spent a small amount of his per diem, so there was enough left for a few drinks. The butterflies in his stomach seemed to be doing a lot less fluttering, so Nick decided that it was a good idea to get something to eat. He knew that as the time drew nearer to the meeting time, the butterflies were going to be much more active. He stopped at a small greasy spoon type of place where you could always count on getting a good burger and fries.

The meal was as good as he had expected and before long he was on the way back to the La Quinta. He looked at his watch and saw that it was already two o'clock. Thinking that it was just a matter of hours now made the burger and fries feel like a huge heavy lump in his stomach.

He got to his room and the first thing that he did was to see if there were any messages on the phone. The little red light just sat there unlit. Nick opened his briefcase and took out his notes. After reading them over, he used a blank sheet of paper and drew an outline of the room and a plan of where the lights, set and camera would best be located. He also brought with him several catalogues of equipment, so he began adding up the figures and writing his report.

~

Lori was equally nervous about the evening. It wasn't only the meeting with Nick, but how she was going to handle the whole cocktail party thing. John was gone since about nine this morning, and since he and Brent had their special presentation this evening before the party, they were going to take off the afternoon and work together to get it ready. Lori was in reading position in her now favorite chair. She was barefoot and wearing her denims and white blouse with the tail out. Next to her was a small bottle of rum from the honor bar and a soda. Nothing fancy about her, she drank enough of the cola to make room for the rum and emptied the miniature into the can.

The door to their room opened and John and Brent entered. Brent's and Lori's eyes immediately met. John, of course, didn't notice or just didn't care.

"Lori, Brent and I are going to his room and work on the presentation. I'll be back in a couple of hours, and we can get dressed." He picked up his brief case and headed for the door.

Brent looked back at Lori one last time before leaving, and smiled. "See you in a few?"

Lori smiled back and nodded.

As always, time flew by while reading and in what seemed like only a short while John entered the room. "I think we're as ready as we're going to be. You want to get ready first or do you want me to?"

"You go first. It'll take me a lot longer."

John went into the shower. *You know, he never even asked to see what I bought to wear tonight. Jesus, he's proven it over and over that he really doesn't give a shit. Why do I always expect something different.* Lori just shook her head and got back into her book until it was her turn to get ready.

John came out of the shower. "See, only one towel. Aren't I a good boy?"

Lori thought that this didn't deserve her time or effort to reply, so she just got up out of the chair and walked past him, picking up her robe on the way into the bathroom. She dried her hair with the blow dryer before she came out. Her long hair was very silky and shiny when she was finished. She was very fortunate to have naturally good skin and features, so she required very little make-up. John was already in his suit and looked quite handsome when he dressed up. It was a shame that he was such a shit. He was engrossed in a sports program on the TV and didn't even notice her as she dressed in her new clothes. She stood behind him and feeling her presence he turned around and saw her.

"Jesus Christ, is that really you?"

"So nice of you to recognize me. Are you ready to go?" Lori decided that she was going to the presentation as well. She wanted to get as much mileage out of her new outfit as possible.

"Lori, you look incredible. I can't believe it. You look like a million dollars."

A million? You'll really think you got a deal when you get the bill. "Believe it, sweetheart. I didn't want to embarrass you in front of your friends. Shall we go?"

"Sure." John just stared at Lori for a few moments, then opened the door and let her go out first.

They went directly to the room where the presentation was going to be made. Brent came over to them and looked at Lori.

"You have to be the most stunning woman in the place tonight," he said as he took her right hand and kissed it.

She felt electricity flow through her body. "You look quite handsome yourself, Brent."

"If you two are finished, I'll show you where to sit," John said to Lori.

There were about one hundred and fifty seats set out in the room. Most of them were occupied. On a raised platform there was a podium, a microphone and two chairs facing the audience. John took her to the front row and showed her to a seat pretty near the middle. Once she was seated, John left her to go over to where Brent and a sophisticated looking older gentleman were standing. She noticed that Brent kept looking towards her and smiling at her. After about ten minutes the older gentleman walked up to the platform with Brent and John following. They sat in the chairs, and the emcee tapped the microphone to see if it was working. The room fell silent. The gentleman gave a brief introduction describing the work that John and Brent were doing and of its importance. Lori had no idea what he was talking about and she fought the urge to turn around in her seat and see if she could recognize which woman in the room might be the infamous Miss Miami. Maybe she wasn't even here and that's why John asked her to come in the first place. Is this her denial side talking right now? Maybe she would ask Brent at the party. Then again, if

Brent wasn't in Miami, how would he know who she was to begin with. She had to stop this insane internal dialogue. Her thoughts turned to the meeting with Nick in just a couple hours. Lori opened her purse and made sure that she had Nick's hotel number. There it was under the small package of tissues. As she regained control of her senses, she noticed that John was already speaking. The rest of the presentation took about an hour and was followed by a loud applause and a standing ovation. She had no idea that his work was so important, but then again how could she? He never talked about work when he was at home. She automatically joined the rest of the group in the standing ovation, and soon everyone was walking out of the room and into another banquet room where the cocktail party was to be held. She patiently stood at her seat while a crowd of people surrounded Brent and John shaking their hands and showering them with praises. Soon, Brent and John were free, and they came over to her.

"Boy am I glad that that's over," John said with relief, "I need a drink."

"Me too," Brent agreed. He turned to Lori and offered his arm. "Can I buy you one?"

"You sure can," Lori answered as she took his arm and went into the banquet hall. John was already there with a large drink in his hand and talking to another small group of men. He didn't even notice Brent and Lori as they passed him, arm in arm, on their way to the bar.

A band was set up and started playing. "What would the beautiful lady like to start with this evening?" Brent asked.

"She would like to start with a glass of champagne."

Brent turned to the bartender and said, "The lady will have a glass of champagne, and I will have a bourbon and Coke."

The bartender quickly filled their order, and Brent put two dollars in the tip glass.

"Shall we go to a quiet corner?" Brent asked.

They found an empty table at the opposite corner from the band. Brent held the seat out for Lori as she sat.

"Lori, you really are a knockout, you know that?"

"You were always the charmer. So tell me, why aren't you escorting a beautiful blonde tonight?"

"To tell you the truth, I've been so busy that there really hasn't been time to find that someone special. Now that the project is finished, maybe I can relax some and see what happens."

"Are you still in a truth telling mode?"

"Depends. Is this something personal?"

"I guess so. Do you know if that girl from Miami is here?"

"Lori, I told you that I wasn't in Miami, so I didn't meet her."

"Didn't John tell you anything?"

"No, but since we're being honest here, I did see a group picture of the trip and the student intern was standing next to John."

"Brent, is she here?" Lori asked very directly.

"I think that's her standing by the fountain."

Lori looked to where the fountain was and saw several women talking. There was only one who was young enough and most likely to be a student intern. She was a leggy blonde wearing a very short red dress. Tears formed in Lori's eyes, and she opened her purse and took out some tissues.

"I'm so sorry, Lori. I don't know what to say. Are you okay? Do you want to go outside?"

"I'll be all right, Brent. Maybe you could go buy me another drink, please? The same."

When Brent came back with the drinks, he saw Lori looking at her watch. It was seven o'clock. "You got a date tonight?" Brent asked.

"As a matter of fact there is something that I have to do shortly. Will you excuse me for a minute? I have to make a call."

"Sure. I'll save your seat."

Lori went back to their room, sat on the edge of the bed and found Nick's number in her purse. The two glasses of champagne blurred her vision, but she made out the number and dialed it. After several rings she heard, "La Quinta. How can I direct your call?"

"Nick Lawson's room please?" Her hand was shaking and she could barely sit upright.

"One moment please while I ring his room."

Nick had been sitting by the phone all evening waiting for it to ring. His stomach was in a large knot. Although expected, the ringing of the phone made him jump.

"Hello," was all that he could get out.

"Nick, is that you? This is Lori."

"Oh my god. Where are you?"

"I'm in my room. The party is going on downstairs, and I left to call you and see if you still wanted to get together?'

"Are you serious? When can you get away?"

"Let's see, it's seven o'clock. How about I meet you about eight? Is that too late?"

"Hell no. I found a nice quiet place for us to have a few drinks and talk. It's the Whispering Wind, not far from the Marriott. Can you meet me there?"

"I guess so. I may have to sober up some before I get a cab. Who knows where I could end up. I can barely understand myself right now."

"I'll be there at eight and watching for you."

"I guess I'll be seeing you in about an hour. It's the Wandering what, again?"

"The Whispering Wind. Got it?"

"Whishpering Wind. Got it. Bye."

Nick wasn't sure at this point if she got it or not, but he couldn't sit in his room one more minute. The clothing that he was wearing seemed to be a bit too casual for the evening, so he changed into what he referred to as his work clothes. This consisted of a nice pair of slacks and an oxford long sleeved shirt and a sport jacket. He was feeling the need for some liquid courage before their meeting, so he headed out to a friendly looking local bar that he passed while looking for the Whispering Wind. Just a couple of shots of Irish whiskey ought to do the trick. The evenings were still cool and there was about a fifteen minute walk to go, so Nick put on his sports jacket before going outside. He double checked to make sure that he had his room key in the jacket pocket and he was on his way.

Halfway between the hotel and the Whispering Wind was Flannigan's Pub. If he couldn't get a shot of Jamesons here, where else besides Ireland could he get one. The front windows were rectangles placed about shoulder height on either side of the door. It was difficult to see inside since there were neon beer signs in each one. Nick opened the door and immediately got hit with the smell of beer and cigarettes. The place was dark and resembled Archie's Place from the TV program, All In the Family. An old guy was standing in front of the jukebox, in all seriousness, conducting the music. Three seats together were vacant at the bar, so Nick took the one in the middle. The bartender came over to Nick and asked, "What's your poison, me friend?"

"I'll have a shot of Jamesons, please."

"From the Old Sod, are ya now?"

"Afraid not."

"Well, at least you have good taste in whiskey. Hey, can one of yoos put another quarter in the box for the maestro? Good man, the maestro. Been coming here since my old man owned the place thirty years ago."

The bartender placed the shot glass on a napkin and poured a heavy shot. "Let me know when you want a re-fill, now."

"Will do." Nick tossed the shot down his neck. *Man, that's some smooth shit,* Nick thought.

"You must really be thirsty. Ready for another?"

"Sure. Thanks." Nick looked at his watch. It was seven thirty. He still had about fifteen minutes before he had to leave. He knocked back the second shot and could feel his courage building quickly. *No wonder the Irish are such good fighters with shit like this.*

~

Lori was feeling a little better, but the room still had a bit of a spin going, so she stayed put for a bit more time. She looked over at the blonde with the short dress. "Brent, you think that Miss Miami over there is pretty?"

"She's all right, I guess."

"Her dress is so tight that it doesn't leave much to your imagination. I wish I was pretty like that. I was once, you know. Now I'm fat and homely looking. That's why John wants someone pretty, isn't it."

"Lori, look at me." Brent took her head between his hands and turned it so that Lori was looking straight into his eyes. "You have to believe me. You are a very beautiful woman. I wish you realized that. You have it all. You're very attractive and smart. I wish I would have met you before John did."

Lori gave Brent a light kiss on the lips. "You don't know how good that makes me feel. Thanks. Do you know what time it is?"

"It's ten minutes to eight. Why?"

"I have to go, Brent. I have an appointment."

"What kind of appointment can you have at eight o'clock at night on a Friday in a strange city?"

"An important one. Please don't quiz me right now."

"You know I'm not going to do that. Can we have one dance before you go?"

"Brent, I'd love to, but I really have to go."

"I insist. Just one and then I'll let you go."

He held his hand out to her. She arose from her chair, and they went to the dance floor for a slow dance. Brent held her close, and she really liked the feel of his strong arm around her waist. As they turned, Lori scanned the room and noticed that neither Miss Miami nor John were anywhere in sight. The music ended, and there was applause. Lori looked up at Brent and asked, "Can you please take me out to get a cab?"

"Sure."

Lori went back to the table and retrieved her shawl from the back of the chair before leaving. There was a cab waiting out front. Lori thanked Brent and entered the cab.

"The Whispering Wind, please."

The cab pulled away as Brent stood there watching it until it disappeared into the night.

Even after three shots of Jamesons, Nick was still pretty much in control and found his way to the Whispering Wind. Thank goodness he did a test run earlier in the day, because things sure looked differently at night. He entered and asked the gentleman at the door for a table for two, not too close to the piano, but from where he could see the door.

"This way please."

Nick followed him past the piano, where the pianist was playing a romantic classic that he recognized but didn't know the name, and to his table.

"Can I get you something?"

"As soon as my guest gets here, we'll order."

"Very good sir," said the waiter.

Nick looked at his watch and saw that it was past eight. He hoped that Lori didn't get there before him, see that he wasn't there and leave, or worse yet, forget the name of the place. At eight fifteen he really began to worry that the whole evening was going to evaporate before his eyes, when he looked toward the door and saw a silhouette of a woman with a beautiful figure and long hair standing there. His heart raced in his chest as he slowly got up from the chair and headed toward the door. *My god, it's Lori*, he thought. Lori saw him coming toward her and she started walking in his direction. Their paces quickened as the got closer until they fell into each other's arms and held each other closely.

"Lori, I can't believe it. It's really you, and you look incredible."

"You look great too, Nick. I would have recognized you anywhere."

"Lori, c'mon. Our table is over there in the corner." Nick held her hand and led her to the table, where he held the seat for her while she sat. "I still can't believe it."

"Me either."

The waiter came over and asked, "Will you order now, sir?"

Nick couldn't take his eyes off of her. He looked at the waiter and said, "How about some nice champagne. We have a lot to celebrate tonight."

"Right away."

Lori looked into Nick's eyes and started to cry. "I'm so sorry. I treated you like shit and never even let you know why."

"We don't have to talk about that right now. Let's have a nice glass of champagne for old times and catch up. If you want to talk about it later, then we can. Deal?"

"A deal," Lori agreed.

Nick took a napkin and dabbed the tears from her eyes. For the next hour and a half they talked of old times and of new times. They compared their hopes and their dreams. They laughed, and they cried. By the time that the bottle was empty, Lori told Nick all about John and the honor for his work and his trophy chick. She told him how it came about that she looked him up in the first place, and how it was Pam's idea. Nick told her about his old family and his new one, and how he had thought of her so often over the years.

Lori drank the last ounce from her glass and said, "Nick, I feel like some fresh air. Can we take a walk?"

"Sounds like a good idea to me." Nick paid the tab and gave the waiter the tip. When he stood up, his legs felt as if he had just gotten off of a boat after a daylong cruise on rough seas. It took a moment to steady himself. He picked up Lori's shawl and wrapped it around her shoulders. Her legs were a little wobbly as well when she first stood up. They walked out to the street and stood there for a moment and took a deep breath. The coolness of the night air felt quite refreshing.

"Where do you want to walk to? I really don't know the area too well," Nick asked.

"Do you know where your hotel is from here?"

"I think so, why?"

"Let's try that route for a start, if it's good for you."

Nick smiled, took her hand and headed for the La Quinta.

CHAPTER 21

By this time both Lori and Nick felt as if they had never lost contact. Conversation seemed to come easily and freely. They started down the street walking side by side and within a block of the Whispering Wind Lori had reached over and took Nick's hand in hers. As they passed under one of the streetlights Nick looked at Lori and saw how the light shined in her long hair and wondered if her hair still smelled the same as he had remembered.

They continued walking, simply enjoying the city and each other's company without either of them saying anything. Lori saw a flashing sign for a liquor store just ahead. "Nick, I know we've both had a lot to drink already tonight, but would you mind stopping at the store up there and getting a bottle of wine? It'll help take the chill off when we get to your place."

"Sure, why not," Nick replied without any hesitation.

An electronic chime sounded as they entered, and the clerk appeared from the back room carrying a box of bottles. "Lookin' for something in particular?" he asked.

"I'd like something a little on the sweet side, like a Rieseling. That sound okay with you?" he asked Lori.

"Sounds like a good choice to me. I'm in a sorta sweet mood right now."

The clerk knew exactly where to go for the wine and brought it to the counter. "That'll be seven dollars eighty nine cents."

Nick took out his wallet and gave the clerk a ten. The clerk gave him two dollars and eleven cents back, put the receipt and the wine in a long, narrow paper bag.

"Yoos have a good evening. Thanks," said the clerk.

Nick put the change into a donation jar that was sitting on the counter for a feline adoption organization called advoCATs, inc. Having three cats sharing his home, and knowing first hand how much quality they bring to his life, he was particularly sensitive to organizations such as these, and besides, how can you resist a picture of a basket full of kittens.

Lori smiled at this act of kindness. It was nice to see someone who cared about other beings other than just ones self. Nick's coattail got in the way of his back pants pocket as he tried to put his wallet back, and as a result the wallet fell onto the floor without Nick or Lori realizing it. The clerk was also unaware, since immediately after the sale he went to the back room for another box of bottles. The electronic chime signaled them goodbye as they left the store. About twenty feet from the liquor store stood a small vending wagon selling churros, a long piece of extruded dough that is fried and sprinkled with cinnamon and sugar, a great Hispanic treat. The vendor was making them right there and the smell caught both Lori's and Nick's attention.

"Do you mind? I am a little hungry. I'll buy this time," Lori insisted.

Nick could only smile as Lori took the two churros from the vendor and handed them to Nick as she took two dollars from her purse and gave it to the vendor.

"Gracias," said the vendor with a nod.

Nick thanked Lori, handed her a churro and they continued down the street enjoying their treats.

Before long they were at the La Quinta and Nick was pulling his key from his jacket pocket and opening the door. His hand was shaking from being cold, nervous, slightly buzzed or maybe all of the above, and as a result it took two stabs at the keyhole before the key went in and the door opened. Lori entered first then Nick.

"Welcome to my casa. Please make yourself at home," Nick greeted.

Lori was pretty sure that it wasn't going to be like *her* home.

"Hey sailor, gonna buy a girl a drink?" Lori asked playfully.

Nick found the corkscrew sitting by the cellophane covered glasses and opened the bottle.

"This must be aged wine," he remarked, "I can tell by the amount of dust on the bottle." He unwrapped the glasses and poured about half a glass of wine in each. There were two chairs in the room, separated by a small round table and lamp. Lori was already seated and still wearing her shawl. Nick handed her a glass and asked, "Do you want me to hang up your shawl?"

"No thanks. It's a little chilly in here. Maybe after the wine takes some of the chill off."

Nick sat in the other chair and took a taste of the wine.

Lori lifted the glass to her nose, swirled the wine in the glass and took a sniff. "Nice bouquet," she remarked with a snobbish tone.

"Nothing but the best for you. By the way, what time do I have to get you back to the Marriott?"

"I'm not worried about it. The party is probably still going on."

"I mean, what time will your husband be expecting you back?"

"He probably won't care. I believe that he'll be tied up, maybe literally, with someone for most of the night. Mind if I kick these shoes off? My feet are killing me from the walk."

"Be my guest."

A Lori lifted each leg to remove her shoes, Nick noticed how beautiful her legs were.

"Now that feels almost better than sex," she said as she wiggled her toes allowing the circulation to return. She picked up her glass, finished what was left and held it out to Nick. "May I have a refill, please?"

Nick happily got up and went to get the bottle. He returned and poured another one for Lori and topped off his glass.

Lori stood up and took off her shawl, revealing her bare shoulders. "Now it's starting to warm up in here. Actually it feels pretty nice." She loosely folded the shawl, placed it on the foot of the bed and returned to her chair.

My god, she's more beautiful now than I remembered. Nick thought as his eyes caressed her shoulders and arms.

"Nick, I'm sorry for the way I left things with you."

"Lori, I accept your apology, and we don't have to discuss it any more."

"No, I want to. You must have been really angry at me, not to mention the frustration, if you know what I mean."

"Yeah, I admit I was pretty pissed, especially when you refused to tell me what I did wrong."

"You didn't do anything wrong, I mean maybe at the time I thought so, but now I see how things can be, and I don't blame you for anything you did or wanted to do."

"I'm not sure I understand."

"I know, I'm a little scattered right now with the wine and all. I really wanted to make love with you that night. You were really special the way you treated me when the rest of the guys would have been happy if I just disappeared leaving no trace. I liked you a lot back then."

"I liked you a lot, too, but I guess you knew that."

"I know. Things were getting pretty hot and heavy and then for some reason I remembered that you were married and how worldly you were compared to me."

"Yes, I was married, technically, but there was no love left. We couldn't even stand the sight of one another. I was living in the basement, for Christ sake. She already had someone on the side. I had no one."

"So I was just a port in the storm for you? Since she had someone, you had to have someone to throw in her face?"

"Absolutely not. You were something special. You were, and are, incredibly beautiful both inside and out. Being around you energized me and just knowing that you were going to be at work when I got there gave me something pleasant to look forward to in my otherwise miserable life. What's this worldly thing all about? I never traveled outside of the U.S."

"I don't mean it in a travel way. The guys used to talk about you and all of your experiences with women, and since I was so inexperienced in those things I was afraid that it I would be really bad and disappointing for you."

Nick couldn't help but laugh out loud.

"Are you making fun of me?"

"Not at all. I just find it funny that I had a reputation that I could only fantasize about. I can't believe that you believed all of that shit.

I'm not the type of person that runs around all of the time in search of babes. As a matter of fact, my past would more likely bore you. How many different women do you think I've been with since high school?"

"You really want me to give you a number?"

"Yes. I'll be one hundred percent honest with you. Take a guess."

"Fifteen?"

"In my dreams. One more try."

"Ten?"

"Lori, two and a half."

Lori had an amazed look on her face.

"A half? Was one of them a guy or something?"

"Christ no! I did some heavy petting with a girl in high school. I guess that counts as half."

They both laughed and drank more wine.

"So, how about you? How many men have you been with?"

"One. John and I made love a couple of times in high school and then there wasn't anyone until he came back after he finished school and we got married. The rest of my experiences have all been my romantic literary rendezvous."

Nick couldn't believe that someone as beautiful as Lori didn't have men falling all over her all of the time.

"Can I use your bathroom?" Lori asked.

"Of course. It's right over there."

Lori got up and steadied herself by holding on to the arm of the chair before heading to the bathroom. While she was gone, Nick divided the last of the wine between their glasses. Lori came out of the bathroom holding her black pantyhose in her hand. She went back to her chair and put them in her purse.

"Now, if you excuse me, I have to get rid of some of this wine to make room for the rest."

When Nick came out of the bathroom, he saw that Lori had already turned the lamp off so that the only light in the room was what was coming from the bathroom. Lori was lying on the bed and motioned for Nick to join her. He tossed his jacket on the floor and got on the bed next to her.

"Nick, this has been a really nice evening. I'm glad we were able to get together."

"It's been really special for me, too."

"Would you mind rubbing my back a little. I'm a little tense." Lori rolled over on her stomach. Nick quickly removed his shoes, straddled her back and started rubbing her shoulders. Her skin was as smooth as silk and wonderfully warm. He could feel himself becoming excited. "It might be easier if you unzip the dress." Now his hands were really shaking as he slowly unzipped her dress all the way down to the base of her spine, revealing her entire back. He opened her dress as wide as he could and placed both hands on her back. He could feel goose bumps form on her skin, and she let out soft moans of pleasure. He continued massaging.

"Am I doing it right?" he asked softly.

"You're doing fine. How about going a little lower."

Nick changed positions and was now sitting next to her and facing the foot of the bed. He repositioned his hands on her back, only now his fingers were pointing towards her feet. He slid his hands down her silky back, and under the opening of her dress. She was not wearing anything under the dress so his hands easily slid over her bare buttocks. Lori moaned a little louder. On the next pass his hands turned inward and down between her legs which parted and enabled him to touch where he had never been before. Lori raised her hips to allow him better access. Lori slowly raised to her knees and pulled her dress over her head and dropped the dress in a heap on the floor. Still on her knees, she turned around to face Nick. There she was, with her long hair falling over her shoulders and resting on her breasts. Nick couldn't believe that this was happening. He quickly undressed and lied down as close as he could to her, wanting to make as much skin to skin contact as possible. They kissed deeply and passionately. He was in an extremely excited state right now, but didn't want it to end yet. He wanted the feeling to last as long as possible. He baby kissed his way across her breasts, across her belly until his nose reached her pubic area. Lori couldn't keep her body from moving. She reached down and felt Nick's excitement growing.

She had an urge to do something that she had never done before and lowered her head to meet her hand.

Suddenly there was an enormous explosion outside that made the windows of his room shake. This startled them both, and they jumped out of bed and held one another tightly. They pulled the blanket off the bed and wrapped themselves in it. The fire trucks, sirens blaring, passed the hotel just below the window and stopped not very far away. Nick and Lori looked out of the window and in the direction of where they had been just an hour or so ago. The sky was bright orange with flames. After composing themselves and thanking god that they were all right, they went back toward the bed. Lori, still naked sat on the edge of the bed silently. Nick turned again to look at the fire raging just a few blocks away. He thought of how close he came to making Meg a widow and his son fatherless. He thought of how much he really loved Meg and questioned what he was thinking to allow what almost happened to happen. Was it the obsession over the years to finish the unfinished symphony? Was it worth the risk of losing everything that he held so dear? Nick was brought back to the reality of the moment when Lori spoke.

"Are you all right?"

"I think so."

"Come over here closer."

Nick, still naked stood in front of her. Lori put her arms around his waist and pulled him closer so that the side of her face was resting just below his navel. Nick gently ran his fingers through her hair.

"You want to get back into bed?" Lori asked.

"I'm sorry, Lori. I can't. I hope you're not too upset. I just can't right now."

"I understand, and I'm not upset. This evening was one of the best that I can ever remember. Maybe I should go now."

Lori picked up her dress from the floor and took it into the bathroom to get dressed. Nick dressed and turned the light back on in the sitting area. The flames were shooting higher in the sky now and more fire trucks were speeding past. Lori came out and put her shoes on. Nick picked up her shawl from the floor by the bed where it had been kicked off earlier. He placed it around her shoulder.

"Can you please walk me down to get a cab?"

"Sure. I'll pay."

"Before I go, do you have a piece of paper? I want to give you my home address and cell phone number, if you want it."

"I do."

Nick went to the nightstand where there was a piece of hotel stationary, an envelope and a pen. He gave them all to Lori. When she was finished, she folded up the paper and sealed it into the envelope. Nick took it from her and put it into his briefcase.

He escorted Lori to the front of the hotel where there was a cab waiting. He reached into his pocket for the cab money and noticed that his wallet was missing.

"I can't find my wallet. I hope I didn't lose it somewhere."

"Well, we know you had it at the liquor store. Why don't you call them in the morning and see if someone found it. Don't worry, I have enough for the cab fare."

"Thanks again, Lori. Can I call you occasionally? I don't want to lose contact again."

"I'll look forward to it."

Nick reached his head into the cab window and gave Lori a kiss on the forehead. She waved as the cab pulled away. Nick went back into the lobby where there were several people gathered watching the fire. Nick went back up to his room and looked at the messed up bed and the two nearly empty glasses. It all seemed like a dream.

~

The cab dropped Lori off at the Marriott. The party was over and the staff was already cleaning up. She looked at the clock on the wall behind the desk and saw that it was one o'clock. As predicted, when she got to her room it was empty. John still wasn't back. She picked up the phone and dialed a number.

"Hello, it's me. Did I wake you up?"

"No, I'm just lying here watching TV. I'm too wound up to go to sleep right now."

"You want some company?"
"Sure. Come on over."
"Be right there, Brent."

CHAPTER 22

Meg was having her morning coffee and English muffin while watching the latest news on CNN. A picture of a serious fire came up on the screen. The announcer read, "Last night two buildings were totally destroyed and at least three people dead from a fire that authorities believe was started by a propane tank explosion. Investigators from the New York City Fire Department believe that a faulty connection on a propane tank on a vendor cart leaked enough gas to be ignited by a small burner inside the cart. At least three bodies have been found in the rubble, but they were so burned beyond recognition that positive identification will have to be determined by dental records.

Meg thought how horrible that would be in D.C. if that happened. Almost every corner in D.C. has one of those carts. Not long after that the phone rang.

"Hello, is this the Lawson residence?"

"Yes it is. Who's calling please?"

"This is Lieutenant Anderson from the New York City Police Department."

Meg immediately thought that Nick was in some sort of trouble. "Is something wrong?" Her heart began to pound in her chest.

"Ms. Lawson, is your husband visiting New York right now?"

"Yes he is. He's there on business and he's coming home today."

"When was the last time you heard from him?"

"I talked to him yesterday morning. Why are you asking me all these questions?"

"I'm sorry, but there was a bad fire in the city last night and we found an ID in the rubble with enough still intact to see his name and address. We haven't positively ID'd the bodies yet and will let you know as soon as we have more information."

Meg slid down the wall and was sitting on the floor crying with the phone in her hand. What she was hearing couldn't really have happened. The cats came into the kitchen when they heard her crying and were there to comfort her as only cats can. She didn't hear the officer when he asked, "Ms. Lawson, Are you all right? I'll have someone sent to your house immediately. I'm sorry."

The officer notified the local police who dispatched the paramedics to check on Meg. When they arrived, she was still sitting on the floor crying with the phone dangling from the wall. Meg managed to give them a name of someone who could come over and be with her, and in the meantime, they administered a sedative and took her to bed.

CHAPTER 23

Nick couldn't sleep the night before so he decided to take a long walk around the city to clear his mind. It was almost sunrise before he could fall asleep, so by the time he woke up it was time to check out of the hotel and head for the train station. It was Saturday, so the trip to Penn Station was a quick one. He slept through his departure time but had no problem in getting a seat on a train leaving for D.C. in about half an hour. He boarded the train and sank into the seat for the three hour ride home. For the first time in a long while he felt relaxed. He worked out most of his emotional conflicts during his walk the night before, so now all he had to think about was the ride home and seeing Meg and the girls again.

Nick fell asleep and woke up when the train stopped in Wilmington. He remembered the envelope that Lori had given him, so he opened his briefcase and took it out and read it.

Dear Nick, Here's my address and phone number. If you're ever in the Lauderdale area and have a few free hours, give me a call. Maybe we can do a symphony together. Have a good life. Lor

Nick smiled and refolded the note and put it into the pocket of his briefcase. Before long, the train was pulling into Union Station. After telling the folks at the hotel about losing his wallet, they agreed to advance him enough cash to get him home and tacked it onto his bill. That gave him enough cash to pay for his parking. All he could think of was giving Meg a big hug and kiss.

It was about three forty five when he pulled into the driveway. Inside, all three cats were with Meg on the bed and as soon as they recognized the sound of Nick's car they sat up and looked toward the door. Meg knew that they always did this when Nick came home, but why were they doing this now? *Maybe,* she thought, *they think it's time for him to be here and they're looking for him.* The thought of never seeing him again made her start to cry again. Just then she heard the door open and a most familiar and wonderful sound.

A SYMPHONY TO FINISH

"I'm home."

Meg jumped out of the bed and ran to Nick, holding him so tightly that he couldn't breath. "They said you were dead! I can't believe it. You're here and you're okay!"

Nick looked at her with a puzzled look on his face. "Dead? Someone said that I was dead?"

"Never mind. You're here and that's all that matters."

All of this time the three cats were rubbing Nick's legs.

"I love you so much!" Meg said through her sobs.

"I love you too," Nick said with tears in his eyes. Then he said, "I brought you something special." He handed her a brown paper bag containing six New York Bagels.

Meg opened the bag, looked inside, and smiled broadly.

"Thanks, sweetie. Sharing one of these with you is the best gift I could ever get."

The End?

Printed in the United States
23516LVS00001B/381